DEAD JACK
AND THE SOUL CATCHER

JAMES AQUILONE

Also by James Aquilone
Dead Jack and the Pandemonium Device (Book 1)
Madness & Mayhem

Websites
JamesAquilone.com
DeadJack.com
Facebook.com/OfficialDeadJack

*For Louis, who has the soul of a ninja.
Sho'nuff!*

Published by Homunculus House
Staten Island, New York

Copyright © 2018 by James Aquilone
Dead Jack ® is a registered trademark of James Aquilone.

All rights reserved. No part of this book may be reproduced or transmitted in any form or by any means without written permission of the publisher.

This book is a work of fiction. Names, characters, businesses, places, events, and incidents are either the products of the author's imagination or used in a fictitious manner. Any resemblance to actual persons, living or dead, or actual events is purely coincidental.

Cover Art by Colton Worley
http://coltonworleyartist.blogspot.com/

Cover Design by STK•Kreations
http://stkkreations.com

Interior Art by Ed Watson
http://edwatsonart.com

ISBN 978-1-946346-06-3 (ebook)

ISBN 978-1-946346-05-6 (paperback)

DEAD JACK
AND THE SOUL CATCHER

HOMUNCULUS HOUSE

Table of Contents

- Chapter One: The Most Dangerous Game
- Chapter Two: Driving Mr. Skeleton
- Chapter Three: Shadows Over ShadowShade
- Chapter Four: A Zombie and a Skeleton Walk Into a Bar...
- Chapter Five: Fairies in the Forgotten City
- Chapter Six: Hammer Time
- Chapter Seven: Hit the Fookin Devil Road, Jack
- Chapter Eight: The Purgatory Island Redemption
- Chapter Nine: Between the Devil and the Broken Sea
- Chapter Ten: An Offer You Can Refuse
- Chapter Eleven: Take This Job and Shove It
- Chapter Twelve: A Not-So-Secret Lair
- Chapter Thirteen: Where Is My Soul?
- Chapter Fourteen: Souls. What Are They Good For?
- Chapter Fifteen: Tripping the Light Fantastic
- Chapter Sixteen: Welcome to Nazi Town
- Chapter Seventeen: Caged Fury
- Chapter Eighteen: Not Another Psycho Nazi Doctor
- Chapter Nineteen: The Devil Wears Nada
- Chapter Twenty: That Darn, Motherfookin Cat
- Chapter Twenty-One: This Is Your Horrible Life
- Chapter Twenty-Two: Deal or No Deal
- Chapter Twenty-Three: How Do You Solve a Problem Like Oswald?

- Acknowledgments
- About the Author

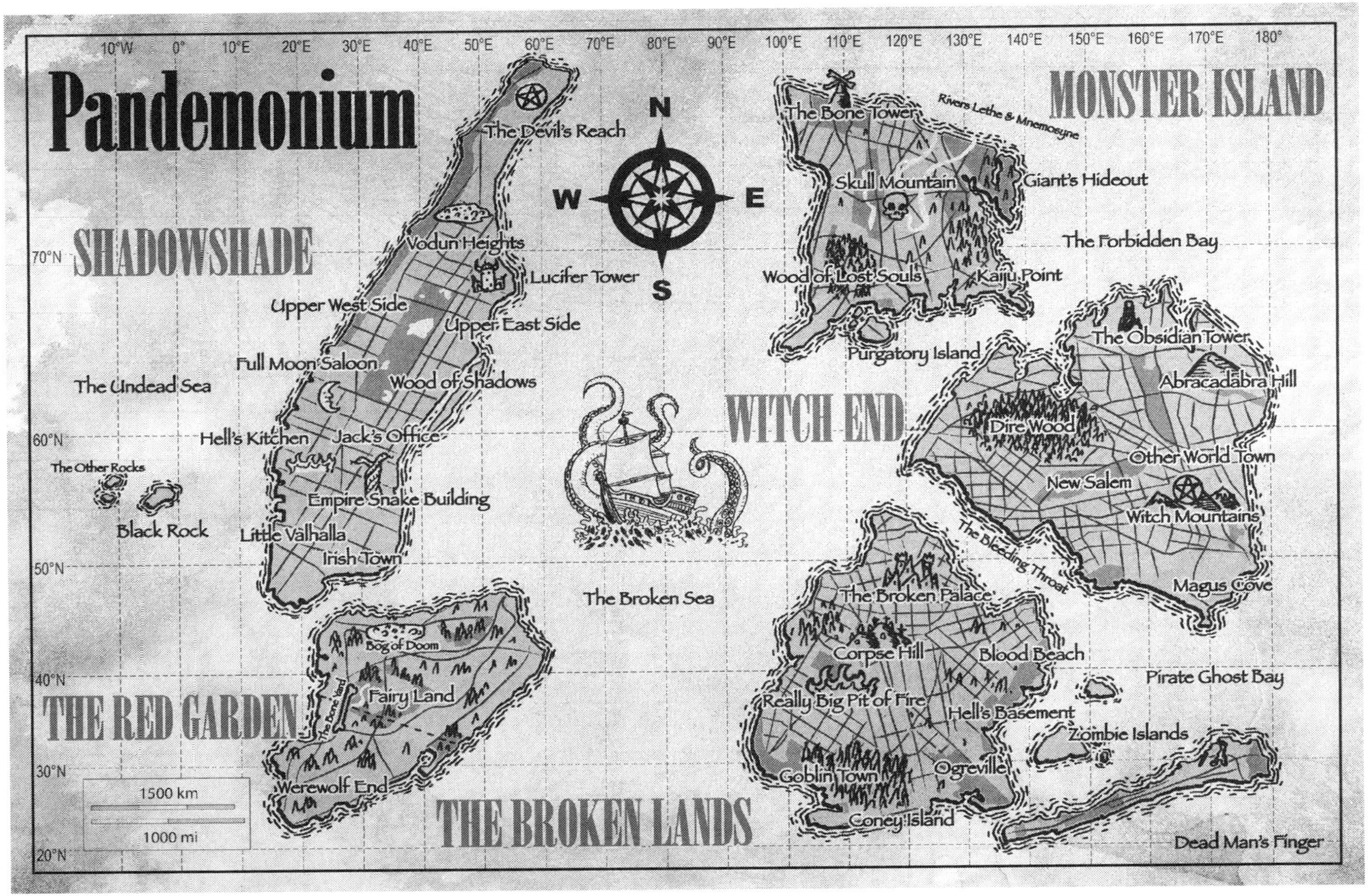
Pandemonium
SHADOWSHADE
MONSTER ISLAND
WITCH END
THE RED GARDEN
THE BROKEN LANDS
N
S
W
E
The Devil's Reach
Vodun Heights
Lucifer Tower
Upper West Side
Upper East Side
Full Moon Saloon
Wood of Shadows
The Undead Sea
Hell's Kitchen
Jack's Office
The Other Rocks
Empire Snake Building
Black Rock
Little Valhalla
Irish Town
The Bone Tower
Rivers Lethe & Mnemosyne
Skull Mountain
Giant's Hideout
The Forbidden Bay
Wood of Lost Souls
Kaiju Point
Purgatory Island
The Obsidian Tower
Abracadabra Hill
Dire Wood
Other World Town
New Salem
Witch Mountains
The Bleeding Throat
Magus Cove
The Broken Sea
Bog of Doom
Fairy Land
The Bone Yard
Werewolf End
The Broken Palace
Corpse Hill
Blood Beach
Pirate Ghost Bay
Really Big Pit of Fire
Hell's Basement
Zombie Islands
Goblin Town
Ogreville
Coney Island
Dead Man's Finger
1500 km
1000 mi
10°W
0°
10°E
20°E
30°E
40°E
50°E
60°E
70°E
80°E
90°E
100°E
110°E
120°E
130°E
140°E
150°E
160°E
170°E
180°
70°N
60°N
50°N
40°N
30°N
20°N

The Most Dangerous Game

A MOLEMAN WITH a smirk as greasy as a succubus's thighs limped out of the shadows and dragged the orc's body toward the back of the Little China dust den. A thick, milky-white liquid rivered out from the gunshot wound in the giant goblin's right temple, leaving an ominous trail on the grimy floor.

I rested on a milk crate in the middle of the room, opposite Carlos, a junkie brownie with a twitchy eye. Between us sat a table covered in fairy dust and around us crowded some of Pandemonium's biggest degenerates. You know, the type of guys who tripped sea hags for laughs. Tonight, the crowd of dragon men assassins, ogre gangsters, and vampire pimps got their kicks betting on which of us idiots bit the magic bullet or won the sparkly powder.

They howled and hollered over the orc's death, but finally quieted down when Frod, the werewolf dust den boss, picked up an enchanted revolver with a ridiculously huge barrel and spun its fat cylinder. He handed the weapon to Carlos. The oversized gun looked like something you'd see in a Looney Tunes cartoon or a novelty shop. I didn't understand how the 'chantment worked, just that it could kill any supernatural stupid enough to be in the way of its blast. And there's no one dumber than me in all of Pandemonium's Five Cities.

With the orc down (as well as three other sad sacks before him), that left Twitchy Eye, and everyone's least favorite zombie detective.

For good luck, I sat the comatose Oswald in front of me. Why not? My homunculus associate hadn't done me any good since he fell asleep at the end of our last case. The runt was due.

Obviously, things hadn't gone well since I returned to ShadowShade a few months ago. I had been on a non-stop dust binge, with shots of Devil Boy thrown in for good measure. I hadn't taken a job since that whole Pandemonium Device business. Oswald was a lump of fluff now. A good for nothing, as usual. But he had zero to do with my decision. I didn't have the heart to bother with the detecting business anymore.

The dust I had gotten from the Goblin Queen went straight up my nose and I didn't have a penny to my name. If I couldn't score any dust, I was as good as dead anyway—after I ate through half of ShadowShade. (Without dust, my zombie hunger takes over, and no one wants that.)

The brownie held the enchanted revolver to his tiny temple with a trembling hand. His left eye blinked rapidly. Either he had some spastic condition or couldn't flirt with a succubus. The sleazeballs placed their bets.

Dark smoke mingled with the stench of death and desperation.

A few minutes later, the werewolf boss held up his hairy paw and shouted, "No more bets!" The horde fell silent.

Russian Roulette is played a bit differently in Pandemonium. Instead of putting one bullet in the six chambers, they start with five. We were down to one now, after the orc, a gnome, a banshee, and a two-headed thing called Gus got carried off by that creepy moleman. He looked like a furless sea otter with eyes like pinpricks. I had no idea what he did with the bodies and didn't care to know. Molemen, I've heard, have weird sexual predilections.

Fat beads of sweat dripped off the brownie's chin.

I blew a kiss at him, hoping to soothe the pipsqueak's nerves. "Nervous, little guy?"

Carlos nodded. His long, pointy nose wagged at me like a crooked finger.

"Don't be," I said. "Your head is so small it'll be like blowing out a dandelion with a howitzer. You won't feel a thing."

Twitch-twitch-twitch. That eye gave me the creeps. "What the fook would you know, zombie?" He practically spit out the words. "Your brain is nothing but dust and snot."

I had never heard that one before. I had to laugh. "Are you trying to send Morse code messages with that eye of yours?"

"After you blow your non-existent brains out, I'm going to take that giant marshmallow of yours and roast him on a stick. Homunculus s'mores sound de-fooking-licious." He rubbed his round tummy to emphasize his lame joke.

"I lied. That Bugs Bunny cannon is going to hurt like a bastard. You're going to have a headache for weeks in the afterlife."

"It's not going to be me, brain licker. It's going to be you." He pointed the 'chanted gun at me. "I'm one lucky son of a goblin. Always have been. I was born the seventh son of a seventh son on the seventh day in the seventh year. I even have seven nipples. I can't lose."

"Seven nipples? Can I milk you? I could go for some chocolate milk."

"Get on with it already!" the fat werewolf shouted. Even with my dulled sense of smell, his fetid breath made me gag like someone dunked my head in a cesspool.

"Pull the trigger already or we'll all blow our brains out!" some creature yelled from the back of the room.

The crowd jeered and hissed. Frod held up a paw to silence the demonic delinquents. "Click-click." He pointed a finger gun at the brownie.

"I need to turn away first," Carlos said. "I don't want this ghoul's ugly face to possibly be the last thing I see. He looks like the offspring of a burnt piece of toast and a giant turd."

I let him have the last laugh, because I figured it would be his last ever.

The brownie turned his head, screwed his eyes shut, pulled the trigger, and—click—the damn runt didn't blow his brains out. The first miss of the night. The others had all gone down on the first try. If Carlos really had some magic mojo, I was in trouble.

The fairy let out a sigh and, with a filthy grin, passed the gun to the werewolf. "I told you I was lucky, you soulless fook."

Frod spun the cylinder and handed me the gun. The dust den dirtbags placed their bets. I removed my fedora, set it beside Oswald—no use ruining a seventy-year-old hat—and raised the gun to my temple.

"Aren't you already dead?" someone from the peanut gallery shouted. Everyone laughed. Har-har-har. What a bunch of morons.

The warm revolver burned my skin. A howitzer blowing out a dandelion. Maybe I should make a wish. A wish that I had never gotten involved with that damn Pandemonium Device. I thought of Ratzinger, but blocked it out. I didn't want that Nazi scum to be my final thought. He had plagued too many of my thoughts. The sick doctor ruled my dreams ever since he'd been resurrected on Pandemonium. Every night, I revisited Room 731 and the terrible things that happened there. But even while awake or high on dust, I felt as if I floated in a dark abyss of despair, more so than usual for a zombie. I thought it might have been because Oswald fell into a coma. I did miss bossing around the homunculus and chiding him for his error-laden reports. (I had even bought the dunzy a dictionary.)

If I was an honest corpse, I'd admit wanting to scramble my brains just to stop the misery. But I'm not, so I won't. It had been an anguishing afterlife these past seventy-two years in Pandemonium. Maybe it was time to go bye-bye.

I wrapped my index finger around the trigger, but that fookin suit of bones showed up before I could squeeze it.

"Jack! Jack! Don't do it! You have so much to live for, buddy!"

Garry stood there waving his arms around like a maniac. The obnoxious twit barged into my office about a week ago, blathering about lost souls. The creep had been watching my office for days and only fueled my already increasing paranoia. I burned through a dozen kilos of dust because of him. I thought he'd been spying for the resurrected Nazi doctor, but he turned out to be another pathetic corpse with a pipe dream. Me and Garry went way back—back to the war where we both served in the U.S. Army as well as Ratzinger's dirty little band of undead brothers.

"Scram, Garry." I jabbed the gun into my skull for emphasis. Calling Garry a zombie would be a bit of an exaggeration. He was the zombie's ultimate nightmare: a skeleton in an ill-fitting zoot suit. The ridiculous bouffant wig on his skull didn't help. "Aren't you due back at anatomy class by now?"

"Jack, pal, please, hear me out."

"How did you even know I was here?"

"Lilith told me. She's worried sick about you. She says you haven't been the same since Oswald died."

My ghost secretary had a big mouth.

"He's not dead!" I slammed my fist on the table. The dust jumped.

"Help me find our souls, Jack, before Ratzinger does. You know what that'll mean, don't you?"

Garry had the biggest and whitest teeth I had ever seen.

"I don't even know if I believe in souls anymore. I've been fine without mine."

"Cripes, you don't look fine to me. You're holding a gun to your head in front of a mound of fairy dust. I'd say you've hit rock-bottom, buddy. You need an intervention. I can get you into a twelve-step program. The first thing you have to do is admit you have a problem."

"The first thing you have to admit is that you're wearing a dead gremlin on your head. I can't take you seriously with that stupid wig, Garry. There's no shame in being a skeleton. Embrace it. You'll be much happier." I wasn't crazy about the purple and black zoot suit either—or the gold watch chain that hung from his belt down to his ankle and back into his side pocket. Real snazzy.

"Does it really look that bad, Jack?" He adjusted the toupee. "It's made of real elf hair. They donate it to skeletons, you know? It's a great program. They use only the best elves. Real top-notch supernaturals. So don't poop on it, alright? If you're going to be that way, I might not tell you how you can revive Oswald."

"Seriously, less talking and more bang-bang," Frod said. "It's like you guys don't even want to blow your brains out. I can have the moleman take your friend into the back room, Jack." His yellow eyes lit up when he said back room and his voice had a tiny bit of mischief that made my skin prickle. I made a mental note not to ever go in the back room.

"Wait, Frod." I lowered the gun. "What was that about Oswald?"

"Now who's stalling?" The brownie stroked his curly brown hair.

"I said I know how we can revive Oswald," Garry said.

"How?" I asked.

"I know a guy."

"You don't know anyone but bad tailors."

"Buddy, I'm no liar. I'm as honest as the day is long."

"Pandemonium days are pretty short. Why didn't you say any of this before, dunzy?"

"I tried back in your office, but you were acting irrational and sweating like a vampire in a cross factory. You kept ranting about Ratzinger. You weren't making much sense, buddy. Quite frankly, you were scaring the bejesus out of me."

He was right. I didn't listen to a word he said that day. I

might have been a little messed up on dust, and by a little I mean a whole lot. I kept seeing tentacles emanating from Garry's hairpiece.

"If you're lying to me," I said, "I'm going to use your bones to beat your damn wig to death."

"Come with me and I'll explain everything."

What did I have to lose? I could always blow my brains out another day.

"Okay, Garry."

"Hey, arsehole, what about the game?" the werewolf boss shouted. "We have bets placed!"

"Get some other loser to fill in for me." I slammed the gun down on the table—and the damn thing went off. Oops! The brownie flew out of his seat and landed halfway across the room, his head fully evaporated from the blast. I warned the dunzy. I guess having seven nipples wasn't so lucky, after all.

In the ensuing commotion, I grabbed my hat, Oswald, and a handful of dust, then hightailed it out of there with Skeleton Garry. I've had much worse ideas.

2

Driving Mr. Skeleton

"**GARRY, IF YOU** turn out to be a Nazi, I'm going to be pissed."

The skeleton tried to ride shotgun, but I pushed him away from the Studebaker. "In the back, boney." I took Oswald out of the shoulder satchel I used to carry him and placed him in the passenger seat.

Garry gave me a queer look. "Lilith said you had a thing for the little guy, but I didn't believe it."

It took all I had not to punch him in the hyoid bone.

I got behind the wheel and started the Studebaker. The jalopy wasn't in such good shape before a crazy leprechaun slammed into it. Now it was a corpse on four wheels. The car coughed to life like a dragon with lung cancer, and I pulled into downtown ShadowShade traffic.

Something in my throat tightened, and my skin crawled with imaginary maggots. The dust in my pocket shouted, "Just a bump, Jack! You know you want it!" I glanced up at the rearview mirror. The sartorial skeleton rubbed his phalanges over his femurs. No dust. Not now. I needed to be clear-headed as I spoke to this assemblage of bones in a clown suit. He looked a bit squirrelly, like the least popular ghoul in cemetery school. My bad feelings about him got badder. Back in the war, Garry had been a bit of a flake, the sort of guy who told knock-knock jokes during air raids.

"You weren't pulling my leg back there, were you, Garry? Because I don't have anything to lose at this point. I will dismantle you bone by bone."

"No, buddy, I'm not pulling your leg. I swear on the Great Unicorn."

"Why so nervous?"

"I've never seen you like this, buddy. You look to be in bad, bad shape. What was that business back there?"

"I don't want to talk about it."

"You were going to kill yourself, take the final dirt nap. Do you have a therapist?"

"I was just trying to get dust."

"That's not how it looked to me. Are you okay? Are you getting enough flesh? You can always talk to me, buddy. I'm here for you."

"You're here for me? You're a skeleton, Garry. It doesn't get much worse than that."

"Yeah, but you didn't find me in a dust den playing Russian Roulette."

"I've been in places that would make you piss yourself. That is, if you still had genitalia."

I drove north on Broadway. The Studebaker glided along the snaking thoroughfare, past the goblin sweatshops and the underground gambling dens run by ShadowShade's most notorious ogre gang; past the bustling pawn shops whose windows advertised gently used wizard wands and amulets that promised protection from any danger; and past the vampire blood banks where down-and-out fangers waited on lines that stretched entire blocks. The Pandemonium sky, as dark as dried blood at a day-old murder scene, lit the nasty little city. Things would get much darker before this ended. Garry's reappearance in my life didn't bode well. I preferred keeping the past in the past.

"Just how are we're going to find these souls?" I asked. "Because, quite frankly, I don't see how in the holy heck we can find them when Ratzinger's been tearing up Pandemonium with no luck. He's even got soul suckers. Nasty creatures. I saw a bunch of them on Monster Island. The souls can be anywhere in the Five Cities, maybe even in the Outer Lands, and if that's the case, they're as good as gone. I don't have the first clue where to look."

"I have the first clue, buddy. Actually, it's a whole lot more than a clue. We don't have to find the souls. Because they've already been found. Do you know what an alchemist is?"

"Aren't they the nut jobs who are always trying to turn lead into gold?"

"They're into a bunch of other stuff, too."

"Like?"

"Souls."

"And you know an alchemist who found the souls."

"That's right."

"And you think he can revive Oswald too."

"Right again. You're a pretty good detective. I don't know what those people are talking about."

"What people?"

"The ones who say you're the worst detective in Pandemonium."

"Can you be more specific?"

Garry didn't answer. I turned and saw him staring into space.

"Hello, Garry. You okay?" I waved a hand in front of his face.

He remained in a trancelike state for a few more seconds before snapping out of it. "Yeah, I'm good. I just got lost for a second. You have quite a reputation, buddy. You seem to have pissed off everyone in the Five Cities."

"You know how it is, Garry. Zombies are the lowest of the low in Pandemonium. They hate to see us shambling around." I hit a pothole and Garry flew up and banged his head on the ceiling. Luckily, his wig cushioned the blow. "But back to this alchemist."

"Can you slow down?"

"I need some dust with a Devil Boy chaser or I'm going to eat half of ShadowShade." I cut off a gorgon on a moped. Thankfully, she wore a helmet. "My office is just a few blocks away. Now get to the point, skeleton, or I'm going to call cryptid protection on your toupee."

"I have the alchemist's journal. He wrote about our souls. He was using them in experiments. We find him, we find the souls, and get him to revive Oswald. I'm sure he can do it."

"Kill two birds…"

"Where?"

"It's an expression, Garry. Is there still a brain in your skull?"

"I haven't checked." He knocked on his head a couple of times and listened. I thought it sounded a bit hollow.

"But you don't know this guy or what he's capable of. This whole thing is just a wish and a pray. If you know he has the souls, why not find him yourself?"

"My brain—whatever's left of it—doesn't work so good, Jack. I have episodes."

"Like a minute ago?"

"Haven't you ever wondered how we continue to exist without our souls?"

"I try not to think about it."

"We're running on the residue left by our souls. It clings to us. It's in our skin and bones. But over time, it diminishes until you're nothing but an empty husk, a grunting, mindless mouth-breather. With all my flesh gone, I'm nearly out of soul residue. I forget things. I get confused. I lose myself. I'm running on fumes here. I need my soul, Jack, so"—he hesitated, stared out the window—"so, I can off myself and be done with it all."

"Wait! You want your soul so you can kill yourself? And I'm the one in bad shape? Just do it now, and save both of us the trouble."

"If I kill myself without a soul, I go straight to the basement of hell. I just want peace, Jack."

"What the fook happened to you?"

The skeleton watched the storefronts whiz by as I weaved in and out of traffic. "I got mixed up with this group in Witch End. It started out okay. They wanted to help other humans in Pandemonium. It sounded like a good idea at the time."

"You're not human."

"Yeah, that's what I learned. In spades. They were using me."

"What for?"

"They plan to take over Pandemonium. They want humans to rule, as they do in the Other World. They're tired of being the low men on the totem pole here. They think this world is immoral and decadent."

"But that's what gives the place its charm."

"They're serious. They're all virgins or celibate. They're real shitheads."

"What's the name of this group?" The bald skeleton hesitated. His bones knocked together. "Garry, you want me to trust you, right?"

He said, "The Children of Thule."

"Sound like Nazis, Garry." He got quiet and ran his phalanges through his elf-hair wig. I turned around. "Garry?" He wouldn't look at me. For a second, I thought he was having one of his episodes.

"They are Nazis, Jack. They're the fookers who revived Ratzinger."

I slammed on the brakes. A few seconds later, the Studebaker decided to stop. "You are with Ratzinger! You fook! You sack of calcium! What is this? A setup? I said you better not be a Nazi. Now I'm pissed, Garry. You pissed me off, and I'm about to get infernal on your goofy arse."

A chorus of honks broke out behind me. I was holding up traffic, but I didn't care.

"No, no, buddy!" Garry said. "I had no idea. I promise. I have nothing to do with them. Anymore. They're the ones who did this to me!"

"Did what?"

More cars honked. Someone shouted.

"Made me a skeleton, Jack. They knew about Ratzinger's army of the undead from back in the war. They want to recreate it. So they brought the psycho back and they've been searching for his souls—"

"Our souls."

"Right, Jack, right. They believe a soul is attracted to its corporeal body and will try to reunite with it. So the psychos cut pieces off my body and, using those soul suckers, flew them around Pandemonium hoping it would attract my soul and give up its location. They didn't stop until they'd completely stripped me. They used me as bait, but it didn't work. I had been their prisoner for years, until I escaped with the alchemist's journal."

"Which means these bastards are after you."

"There are a few more complications."

Through the rearview, I watched an ogre exit his truck and head toward the Studebaker. I rolled down my window and started to shout at him to go around when the worst migraine I've ever suffered ripped through my skull. It felt like a dwarf had gotten in there to dig for treasure with an icepick. The ogre stopped at my door, shouting, but I didn't hear a word. I grabbed both my temples as a crackle of static roared in my head. Low and indistinct, the sound buzzed like a radio tuned to a dead station. Was Ratzinger trying to break into my mind? It wouldn't be the first time. I pressed my knuckles into the sides of my head.

The ogre—an ugly green creep with purple sores around his thin lips—reached through the open window and grabbed the front of my shirt. I had enough sense to step on the gas. The ogre's hand slammed against the window frame as I sped away.

"Piece of dead garbage," he growled.

I gritted my teeth and tried to concentrate on the road as a swarm of bees bounced around my skull.

Garry patted me on the shoulder and mouthed something. I couldn't hear him. I think he asked if I was okay.

"I just need to get some dust and formaldehyde in me," I said, probably much louder than necessary, and hoped I'd make it to the office before I cracked up the Studebaker or cracked open my head.

Shadows Over ShadowShade

THE STUDEBAKER SCREECHED to a stop in front of 666 Fifth Avenue. The noise in my head had resolved itself into a dull hum.

Garry's voice broke through the buzzing. "Buddy, buddy, buddy."

I grabbed Oswald, stumbled out of the car, and headed into the building.

As the elevator ascended, Oswald seemed to jump inside the satchel. I took him out, but he looked as dormant as ever, his little "X" eyes and mouth frozen, his body as limp as wet dough.

The elevator banged to a stop at the fifth floor. The static in my head crackled back to life. Was someone talking under the white noise between my ears? I tried to concentrate, but couldn't make anything out. Garbled and distorted, it sounded like a record playing backwards.

"It's a bit dark, isn't it?" Garry said as we stepped into the hallway.

Shadows covered the corridor. A sliver of weak light outlined my front office door at the end. Lilith must have left it open, after she blabbed to Garry about me being at the dust den. The buzzing in my head had me so batty that I forgot Lilith didn't open or close doors—despite my protestations. She always went through them.

The office gave me a bad feeling. I stood outside the door, not knowing whether I should run for a bottle of Devil Boy or bolt out of the building. Garry had no reservations. The skeleton pushed past me and entered the reception area Lily haunts during business hours. She wasn't there at this late hour. I followed, and the moment I stepped past the threshold, the hum turned into a confusion of sound, like a thousand voices shouting at once.

"Nice place, buddy," Garry said. "It could use a little light though."

We crossed the room and entered my office.

I needed to clear my head. I moved toward the bathroom, which I used primarily to glare into the mirror while contemplating the nature of damned souls and the depths of my self-loathing, but stopped.

Usually the desk lamp stayed on, but someone had turned it off. The light from a street lamp filtered through the window blinds, throwing dark bands against the walls.

"Do you feel that?" Garry's teeth chattered. "It's damn chilly in here?"

A breeze as cold as a yeti's nut sack on Christmas morning swept through the room, but a glance at the window confirmed it remained shut.

I tapped Garry on the shoulder and pointed at the walls. Shadows clung to them like hungry spiders.

"Garry, you said your brain doesn't work so good. How about your fists?"

"I can take care of myself."

The room came alive. Shadows slid along the floorboards, puddled in the corners, crawled across the file cabinets. A black-as-midnight shade spread like an oil spill over my desk.

We stood back to back in the middle of the room. The noise in my head had suddenly gone silent.

"What do you know about shadow men?" Garry asked, his voice filled with terror.

"Is this a test, Garry?"

The oily shade detached itself from my desk, and its nebulous, insubstantial form stretched and coalesced into the shape of a wolf. The shadow-wolf pounced, knocking me straight back onto the floor.

It leaped onto my chest and chewed on my arm, which I had the foresight to throw over my precious throat.

I turned to Garry, who ran around the room swatting at shadow-ravens. I didn't know much about shadow men, and I'm dumb as dirt, but I'm a genius compared to him.

"Turn the light on, Garry! They're fookin shadows!"

The shadow-wolf was doing a number on my jacket. I tried punching the shadow, but—wouldn't you know it?—my fists went right through the bastard.

"Good thinking." The skeleton ran in circles. "Where's the light switch, buddy?"

"On the fookin wall, Garry! Like all light switches."

"What?"

"The wall! The fookin wall." I reminded myself his brain wasn't so good.

The switch didn't work.

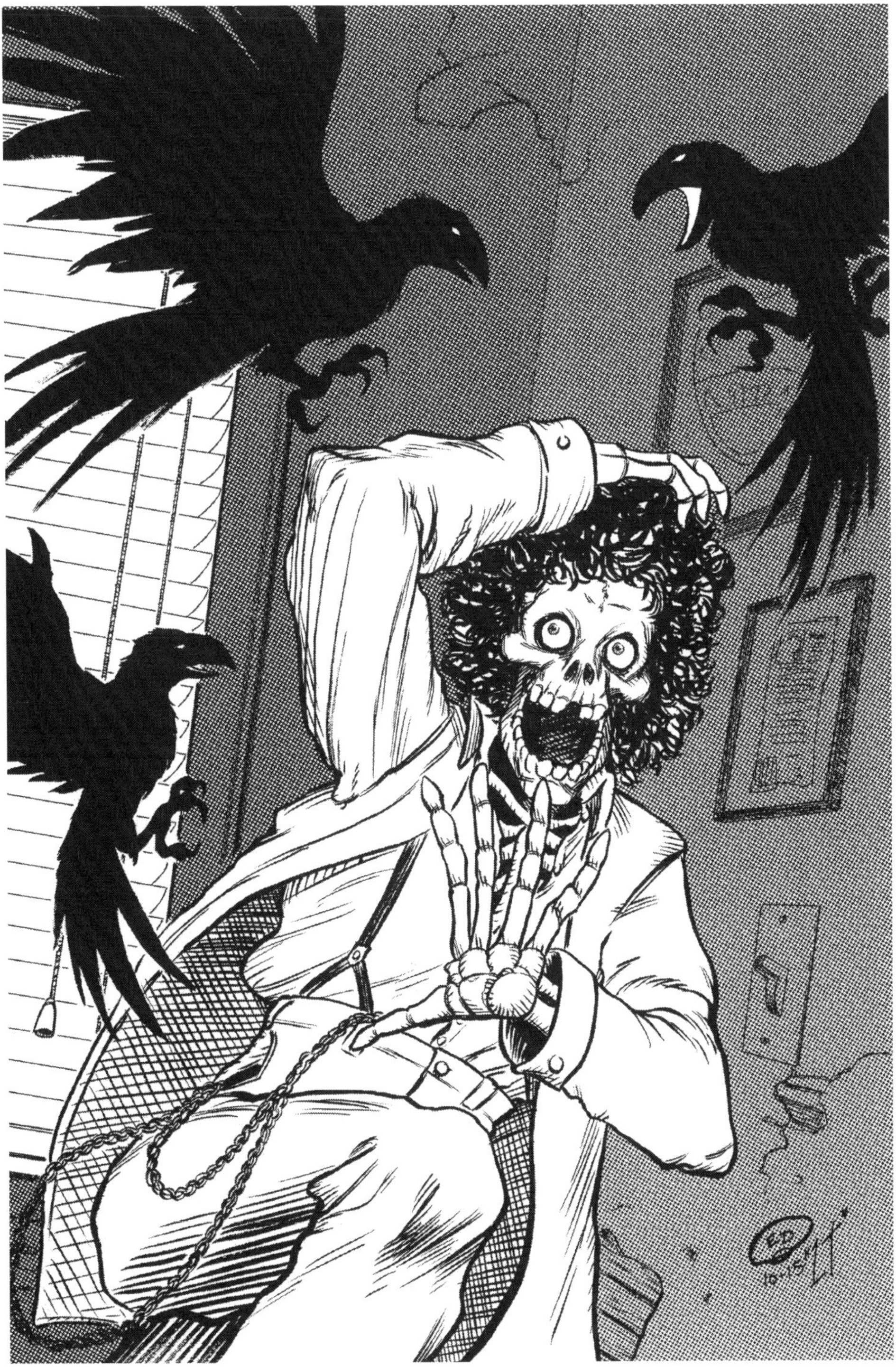

"I think it's broken!" he said. "Did you pay your electric bill?" A shadow-raven pecked at his head, but Garry continued to flick the light switch up and down, uselessly.

I wondered why the shades weren't doing much to attack Garry, other than a few pecks. When I reached into my inner jacket pocket for my lighter, I learned why. The shadow-wolf's lower end morphed into a claw. The creature snatched my satchel, morphed into a shadow-raven, and flew for the door.

"They're after Oswald!" I shouted as I struggled to stand.

Without missing a beat, Garry whipped out his gold pocket watch, held it up at the perfect angle to catch the light coming through the window, and aimed it at the fleeing shadow-bird. Seconds before it reached the door, the creature blew apart in a puff of black smoke. The satchel thudded to the ground.

I scooped Oswald up with one hand while turning up my lighter with the other, the flame dancing in the darkness like the first rays of dawn. I grabbed some papers off my desk—bills, I hoped—and hastily rolled them into batons, which I lit. I gave one to Garry and took another for myself. I waved my makeshift torch at the shadows.

They howled, but got the message and fled the office.

"We should get out of here," Garry said.

"One second." I pulled a painting of three gremlins playing poker off the wall, revealing my safe, and spun the dial left-right-left. The door opened. I grabbed The Book of Three Towers from inside. I had a feeling we'd need some magic.

We headed to the city's worst bar for much needed refreshments.

4

A ZOMBIE AND A SKELETON WALK INTO A BAR...

IF YOU DIDN'T know the Full Moon Saloon was a bar, you'd probably mistake it for a cavern where junkie molemen lived. Dark, spacious, and reeking of raw sewage, the dive bar stood on the ashes of a dozen other dive bars that had all occupied the same plot of land. Each establishment burned down under mysterious circumstances, mostly involving insurance fraud or bad pyrotechnics from the resident band. In the Other World, a Hell's Kitchen bar sat in the same location. Some things never change.

Tonight, an old client, Unicorn de Havilland, provided the musical entertainment. Her trademark was the ivory horn on her head and her racy lyrics. A few years back, I helped her out of a sticky jam. I had heard she broke up with her band, Kill Unicorn Kill, since then. I never cared for her music. It resembled Benny Goodman's work—if Benny had half his brain scooped out.

I hated everything about the place, but the saloon's formaldehyde shots cost half the price of any other bar in ShadowShade.

"What are you drinking these days, Garry? I remember you used to throw back Devil Boys like a champ."

We sat in the booth farthest from the stage, but Unicorn's racket of discordant trumpets and pounding drums still punished my eardrums. She screeched about riding a sphinx over the Broken Sea. I think it was a sexual innuendo.

"These days, milk," he said.

I placed Oswald on the table. "For the bones."

"Yeah, the bones. They're all I've got now." He grimaced and looked down at the table. This guy might be the only person in Pandemonium sadder than me.

I snorted a tiny bump of the dust I had taken from the Russian Roulette game.

"That stuff'll melt what's left of your brain," Garry said.

"How do you stop from feeding?" I asked.

"Since I've gone skeletal, I haven't had to worry about that. I don't hunger. In fact, I don't feel much of anything anymore."

"Try a little dust. It'll make you feel something. But you'll have to get your own. I'm running low."

I waved over the waitress, a cute pixie with purple hair. I knew her well. Gwendolyn hired me a while back to save her daughter from an amorous ogre. She's despised me ever since.

"Gwen, give me half a dozen shots of Devil Boy," I said, "and a tall glass of unicorn milk for my associate."

"We don't serve your kind around here," the pixie said, with a sassy look.

"How adorable, a teeny tiny zombiphobe." The dust

warmed the sludge in my veins, turning it into molten molasses. My migraine dissolved instantly. "You people make me sick, you know that? Isn't life terrible enough without all the hate?"

The pixie looked insulted. Her wings twittered. "I don't have a problem with the undead. I have a problem with deadbeats. We have a wee policy here: bums don't get served. And you, Jack, are one of Pandemonium's biggest bums."

The dust reached my toes. They tingled like carbonated water invading my capillaries. My hunger for sweet flesh dissolved as swiftly as a snowman in hell. At that moment, I almost didn't feel like a zombie. "I've been experiencing financial difficulties ever since I saved the world."

"Bludletter says you're cut off. You can talk to him if you want." Gwen smiled.

Bludletter, the captain of Pandemonium's fastest rising vampire gang, recently took control of the Full Moon Saloon. He'd forced out the werewolf clan that had owned it since they landed in this godforsaken dimension. He had a reputation for impaling his victims with straws and drinking their blood.

"How is Bludletter? Still extorting garden gnomes?"

Garry stood. "I'll take care of it, buddy." He reached into his pants pocket. "How much does he owe?" The skeleton dropped several large gold coins on the table.

The pixie's eyes lit up. "This should cover it. Half a dozen shots of Devil Boy and a glass of milk, right?" She scooped up the coins and headed to the bar.

"Where did you get all that money?" I asked.

"I stole it from the Nazis."

"Garry, did you take the damn swastikas too? Are you crazy? Don't answer that. I know the answer. What I don't know, is how in the holy heck a dunzy like you pulled off that sweet move with the pocket watch."

Gwen came back with the Devil Boy shots and a tall glass of milk.

"I'm not always such a palooka," Garry said. "Sometimes, the old me shows up." He sipped his milk, the frothy white liquid pouring down his throat and into his ribcage. I wasn't sure if that was the old Garry or the new Garry.

"You sure you don't want a splash of Devil Boy in your milk, Garry? We just had a heck of a fright back there."

"That business? That was nothing."

"I thought I saw your bones knocking together."

"Shadow men don't scare me. The Children of Thule scare me."

"You think those shadow men were sent by the Nazis?"

"No. Shadow men are under Lucifer's control. It's said they're the emanations of the dead in hell."

"That's what they say, huh?" I asked.

"They also say Lucifer can leave Pandemonium whenever he wants, but he'd rather rule here than serve Satan in hell."

"You're a big expert on shadow men and Lucifer?"

"They attacked the Children of Thule not long ago."

"How did that go?"

Garry shook his head. "It didn't happen. The Nazis set up a magical block to keep them out of their camp."

"And why would Lucifer attack the Nazis?"

"I have no idea. But they barred him from entering their camp. Why would Lucifer want Oswald?"

I downed three shots of Devil Boy in rapid succession, coating my throat with the chilled formaldehyde. That Lucifer owned the Devil Boy brand wasn't lost on me. He made Lucky Dragon hellfire sticks, too. Lucifer Corp. pretty much owned Pandemonium. You could call him the Nelson Rockefeller of the Five Cities, only he had more ethics.

"Beats me," I said. "He's just a ball of fluff."

"How did that happen?"

"He was sitting on top of a Jupiter Stone when it exploded."

Garry might've tried to blink. "A Jupiter Stone? Aren't they pretty powerful?"

"Seeing as the cyclopses made them from Zeus's thunderbolts, I'd say they pack quite a wallop."

"What was he doing on top of a Jupiter Stone?"

"Saving all us poor schmoes from annihilation. Haven't you heard of the Pandemonium Device?"

"Can't say I have."

"The newspapers wouldn't run the story," I said. "They couldn't believe a zombie saved the world."

"I thought you said Oswald saved the world."

"It was my plan." My stupid plan to have Oswald cover a device powered by an indestructible Jupiter Stone. The Duke built it to destroy the barrier between Pandemonium and the Other World, good old, regular Earth. It would have destroyed our shadow dimension in the process, as well, but the Duke wanted out so bad he didn't mind a little genocide. Like the rest of us, he'd been trapped in Pandemonium ever since the Allies sent us supernaturals here at the end of WWII. We're all a little stir-crazy.

I gulped down another three shots. The Devil Boy combined with the dust to wrap me in a warm blanket of oblivion.

"Feeling good, buddy?" Garry asked.

"Feeling nothing at all." I smiled, but I must have looked like a maniac, because Garry averted his eyes and took a long sip of milk, most of which splashed the front of his shirt. "How did you fall in with those Nazi bastards?"

"I didn't know they were Nazis at first. They seemed like a nice bunch of humans concerned about Pandemonium. They wanted to make things better. At least, that's what they said."

"Oh, no. Don't tell me the Nazis lied?"

"They said they could make me human again. They were doing experiments."

"How cliché. Nazis and experiments, really? I bet they have snazzy uniforms too."

Garry clicked his big white teeth. "You wouldn't believe the meetings about the uniforms. They went on and on. Should they have pinstripes or lightning bolts? They fought over buttons. Buttons! It was crazy."

"You can't destroy a world without looking good."

"I was desperate, Jack. Things have been rough since I got to Pandemonium. I never had it as good as Dead Jack, zombie detective."

"I've never had it good. I just don't let people push me around."

"Then you know how I felt. When the Children of Thule brought me in, I fell for it hook, line, and stinker. But all I got was a cage and frequent meetings with a Nazi butcher. I might as well have been back in Room 731."

"The good old days." I lit a Lucky Dragon, the black smoke gathering like a funeral pyre. "Did you ever see Ratzinger?"

Garry took a gulp of milk.

"Fortunately no. When I heard they planned to resurrect him, I prayed for them to give me the absolute death, even without a soul."

"Why do they call themselves the Children of Thule?"

"The Thule Society was a secret brotherhood that formed after World War I and eventually supplied the Nazis with all its crazy ideas about the master race, the swastika, and the occult. They're the source."

"And they're bringing it all back?"

"Yeah."

"What about this journal?"

"I heard they had found it and believed it would lead to our souls. That's when I knew I had to get my hands on it and escape. Once they had fully stripped me, they didn't bother with me much. I got to roam around the camp a bit, which made it easier to escape."

"And what were those complications you were talking about? You still have the journal, don't you?"

"I've got it, but I can't read it."

"Are you illiterate, Garry? How did a dunzy like you get in the Army?"

"I can read fine, but it's written in a magical language. I've taken it to a bunch of folks and none of them could read it."

"A bunch of folks? How many people know about this book?"

"Not many. Just the Children of Thule and about a dozen wizards, witches, warlocks, and sorcerers."

"How the fook did you get this far, Garry?"

"I guess I'm just lucky."

"Dumb luck. So if you can't read the book, how do you know the alchemist has the souls?"

"There are pictures."

"I can't believe I listened to a burnt-out, toupee-wearing skeleton in a zoot suit."

"Look, Jack." Garry pulled out a ratty, leather-bound book from his jacket pocket. Despite the ridiculousness of his get-up, I had to admire the size of the pockets. Good thing my inside pocket was magical or I'd never be able to fit all my junk in it. He thumbed through the book and handed it to me. I didn't recognize the writing—nothing like the Enochian I saw in the Duke's palace. This language looked like Egyptian hieroglyphics took inappropriate liberties with Norse runes. The right-hand page had a detailed sketch of several egg-shaped vessels. I was about to dismiss the drawing until I spotted the numbers etched on one of them: 1-1-3-4. The prisoner number Ratzinger had given me.

"See. I told you, Jack. Those are our souls."

"Don't get all cocky now, Garry. We're still far from getting our hands on the souls. All we have is a drawing in a book we can't read."

"Those are the souls! He's got them! The Nazis thought the book was important."

"Why didn't they get it translated?"

"They couldn't figure out the language either. Besides, they had it for only a few days before I took it."

"And you think I can find a translator?"

"Can't you?"

"You really are one lucky son-of-a-corpse. I know just the person."

"Who?"

"There are some complications. Finish your milk. You're going to need strong bones." I downed my three remaining shots of Devil Boy. My body felt electrified and the bad thoughts and feelings buggered off. I jumped up and shouted, "I'm ready to get this adventure started!" then fell flat on my face.

"Buddy, I don't think you're in any shape to drive."

I looked up at the skeleton. "I've never felt better."

5

Fairies in the Forgotten City

"HAVE YOU EVER broken someone out of prison?" Garry asked after we boarded the ferry to the Red Garden.

My dust and Devil Boy high had already started to wear off. The brightness in the world faded, my body cooled. Still, I felt a ton better than Garry. I had no idea if a skeleton could vomit, but he sure seemed to be doing his best. Garry bent over the railing, convulsing and shaking as if trying to dislodge something from this throat.

"You shouldn't have drank all that milk, Garry."

"You could have let me know we were taking a cruise."

The ship, if it could be called that, perched upon the back of a giant orange sea turtle named the Spirit of Pandemonium. At least it beat a ghost ship. As water travel went, the ferry wasn't too bad. A forecastle where passengers could sit and eat had been built atop the middle of the turtle's back. It even had a snack bar that served stale mead and ancient hot dogs.

We stood on the outside deck as the turtle navigated

the choppy waters. Downtown ShadowShade drifted away behind us, a shining jewel surrounded by darkness.

I stared out at the black water leading to the Red Garden. My last cruise didn't go so well. I ended up nearly drowning and getting molested by a shark woman. But that's what you get when you sail with pirate ghosts, or ghost pirates. I still haven't figured that one out.

Garry stopped retching and I led him back into the sitting area. Fairies filled the room, along with a few goblins and gremlins. War propaganda posters covered the walls. "Loose Lips Sink Ships." "Stay Vigilant." "The Big Bad Wolf Is Out to Get You."

Fairies and werewolves don't get along. The two groups have been at war since they both set foot in The Red Garden, which gets its name from all the blood spilled there. I had no idea why they bothered to fight over a godforsaken island of swamps and grasslands. It's pretty much the same back in the Other World, where it's called Staten Island.

"Are you going to be okay, Garry? I'm not a big fan of the sea either."

"It'll pass. I just need to sit down."

We sat in the middle, away from the other passengers, who all clustered around the windows and watched the waves slam against the turtle's side.

"You didn't answer my question," Garry said. "Have you ever busted anyone out of prison?"

"I've busted people out of lots of places. It's second nature to me."

"This is Purgatory Island we're talking about. People don't just go waltzing in and out. You can't even use magic inside."

Garry had a point. We weren't going to have an easy time of it. Dark elves guarded the maximum-security prison and a magic inhibitor made any funny business impossible there.

"You said no one can translate the alchemist's journal," I said. "But I know a guy who can."

"Waldo?"

"Wallflower, but everyone calls him Wally. He's an expert on magical languages as well as Pandemonium's greatest sorcerer."

"If he's such a good sorcerer, why is he in prison?"

"He's a great sorcerer, but he's not such a great person. Wally got pinched for selling fake philosopher stones. The judge sentenced him to one year to infinity. Frankly, I think it was a bum rap."

"If you say so, buddy. I trust you." Realization finally hit the skeleton. His eyes bulged. "Hey, but aren't we going in the opposite direction of Purgatory Island?"

"We need to make a pit stop. Like you said, we can't just waltz in. We need backup."

"I think I'm gonna be sick," he said before scurrying to the railing. No, a skeleton cannot vomit. It was all in his head. Garry had lost his mind. He'd be no help on the mission. I just hoped my old pal had forgiven me.

The turtle thumped to a stop at the northern end of the Red Garden a half hour later. We disembarked, wading through the sea of fairies and sticking out like sore thumbs. Garry was still a little shaky from his pretend puking fit, so I had to practically carry him off the turtle.

"Who's the guy that's going to back you up?"

"It's not a guy, you sexist pile of calcium. Her name is Zara Moonbeam."

"A woman?" The skeleton laughed, a chattering teeth kind of laugh.

"Garry, you impressed me with that watch bit, but you're a glorified Halloween costume. And you've got that not-so-good brain. You're going to be as much help as Oswald here." I patted my satchel.

"What did you do back in the office, except get knocked down by a shadow? I saved your desiccated arse."

I took out a Lucky Dragon and lit it. "Garry, I'm going to pretend you didn't say that."

"I still don't see how a teeny, tiny pixie is going to be of much help."

"Zara's a six-foot pixie-slash-witch who swings an enchanted sledgehammer like she's Thor himself. I wouldn't laugh around her unless you want to be pulverized into dust."

We stood at the taxi stand, trying to wave down a ride, but all the fairy cabbies passed us by.

"No one likes to pick up a zombie," Garry said, "especially in Fairy Land."

"You're not helping matters with that wig. They're probably afraid you'll infest their cab."

A big yellow taxi slowed down as it approached—but the driver hit the gas when he saw us, and left us choking on fumes. A few minutes later, another cab pulled up.

The driver, a rough-looking gnome with a thick cigar dangling from his mouth, rolled down his window. "Where to, ghouls?"

"I'm trying to find an old friend, Zara Moonbeam," I said. "Do you know where I can find her?"

His eyes bugged out, all the color drained from his cheeks, and he zoomed off without uttering a word.

"Maybe we should walk?" Garry said.

"Great idea. Except I have no idea where I'm going."

I managed to flag down another cab. "Can you take us to Zara Moonbeam? I don't have an address."

"Why would I do that?" the cabbie asked.

"Because I'll pay you. That's how it usually works."

"All the money in Pandemonium couldn't get me to go there."

"Where is that?"

"The front lines, ya idjit. General Moonbeam leads the fairy army. Don't you read the papers?"

"General, huh? How about I give you a bag of dust?"

"Fairy dust?" He burst into laughter, a sound like bubbles bursting.

I dangled dust in front of people so often I forgot where I was.

"This is Fairy Land, idjit. We're swimming in dust here. Find yourself another ride." The cab vanished amid a squeal of tires.

We walked down a narrow dirt road leading away from the ferry terminal. It wasn't much more than a rut. Like I said, the Red Garden is the sticks. I could smell the swamp from here. Like rotten eggs covered in damp towels. Only a few buildings dotted the landscape, mostly of the mushroom variety.

A procession of fairies trooped up beside us. They wore green armor that sparkled in the light and carried tiny swords that resembled those cocktail picks they put olives on. They were also drunk out of their minds.

The fairies staggered down the road, banging on drums and making merry. They tumbled, swayed, and hopped, shouting, "Who's afraid of the big bad wolf, the big bad wolf?"

Dead Jack and the Soul Catcher

One of the fairies yelled, "Out of the way, brain lickers! We are the Fifth Regiment of the Fighting Pixies. Undefeated in battle. Undeterred and determined. We're to be feared and respected." He belched. It smelled like grass and whiskey.

"What are you drinking?" I asked.

"Morning dew and Dewars," the fairy said. His helmet, two sizes too big, jangled and shook on his head as he wobbled down the path.

"I am a friend of your General Zara Moonbeam and I have very important information to convey to her."

"A friend of General Moonbeam's, you say? A ghoul? Not likely." The fairy looked me up and down. He seemed sober for a moment and the look in his eyes frightened me. "I remember one of your kind a while back who ate two dozen fairies. Do you remember the affair?"

I broke out in a sweat. It was actually only one dozen. These things get so blown out of proportion. And I wouldn't have called them the nicest fairies in Fairy Land. As I recall, they were zombie-hating jerks. Still, the incident was one of my low points, and I've made a habit of having low points. Oswald made me vow to give up flesh after the incident, a vow I intend to keep unless I have no other choice or the creature deserves it.

"It doesn't ring a bell," I said. "I don't get around to these parts much. I'm more of a city boy."

"I think the ghoul's name was Dick. Dick Jack?" He looked me up and down again, but the bloodshot eyes glistened and worked hard to focus. If the fairy hadn't been drunk out of his mind, I might have been in trouble.

"Hey, don't they call you the Dead D—!" I jabbed Garry in the ribs before he could finish his sentence.

"Dick Jack," I said. "I think I heard someone ate him not too long ago."

"Serves him right," the fairy said. He hiccupped as if he had a squeak toy lodged in his throat. "And what's your name?"

"John. John Colombo."

"I am Oren Nero, commander of the Fifth Regiment of the Fighting Pixies."

"So how about taking us to the general?"

"I don't traffic with ghouls."

"I'll let General Moonbeam know you failed in your duty to protect Fairy Land."

"I'm not falling for that one. You have to wake up pretty early to fool the likes of me."

"This man here." I pointed at Garry. "Is a casualty of war. All his flesh was eaten by weres."

"You don't say?"

"I do say. Garry here killed three of those shifty animals in the commission of a battle, but not before the damage was done."

The fairy studied Garry. "A war hero." He nodded. "And a mighty fine dresser to boot and hair like an elf." He seemed impressed. "Follow us. We're heading to the Bone Yard."

We went marching south, singing, "Who's afraid of the big, bad wolf? Big, bad wolf, big, bad wolf?"

South of the Bog of Doom, we came upon the remains of a battle. Bodies of fairies and werewolves mingled with each other on the bloody ground.

"Lucky for you, ghoul," Oren Nero said. "Looks like we just missed a heck of a row."

The air stunk of blood and wet dog.

A few of the victorious fairies dug ditches to bury their dead.

Dead Jack and the Soul Catcher

We marched through the field and got a closer look at the carnage. Most of the dead shifters lay in human form, their naked bodies cut in half at the torso or decapitated. The fairies looked like old chew toys. I didn't know how Zara got mixed up with all this. The pixie/witch had told me she was heading to the Red Garden to reconnect with her estranged mother.

As we approached the Bone Yard, the stench of rotten flesh grew more intense.

Oren Nero said the fairies were winning the war after many years stuck at a stalemate. Ms. Moonbeam, according to him, had tipped the scales in their favor. She had tallied victory after victory against the wolves and recently pushed them back to the edge of the Bone Yard, which got its name for all the bones buried there, fairy and werewolf alike.

We entered an encampment, which sat a few miles from the edge of the Bone Yard. Tiny tents dotted the area. Fires burned. Fairy soldiers scuttled about. The hills of the yard lay beyond the camp like the back of a giant white kraken. Carrion birds circled overheard. The place stunk worse than the Zombie Islands.

The commander took us to the largest tent. He signaled for us to wait a few paces away and approached the two fairies who stood guard. He whispered in one's ear. The guard looked me up and down before nodding. The commander walked back over to us.

"General Moonbeam will give you an audience."

"Thank you, Oren Nero." I bowed.

When the trooping fairies left, I said to Garry, "Don't say a word about Zara not looking like a pixie. She's pretty sensitive about it."

"Why would she want to look like a pixie?"

"On second thought, don't say anything about anything. Let me do the talking."

The fairy guard pulled aside the tent flap and waved us inside, smirking. "Stay vigilant."

A deafening roar caught me off guard as I entered the tent. I turned to my left. Blazing eyes and wet teeth emerged from the darkness. Hair and claws. I jumped back, but apparently not far enough—clawed hands seized my throat.

Garry screamed, "Weres! Weres!"

Did the fairies set us up? What the fook was going on?

A commotion spread over the camp, fairies yelling and running. The werewolf's powerful hands tightened around my throat. I gagged.

Zara's voice rang out over the din. "Can someone, please, remove that zombie from the werewolf?" She sounded much calmer than I expected.

A tiny fairy fluttered toward us with a stick in his hands. When he got close, he poked the stick behind me. It let off a zap and the werewolf howled. The creature released his grip on me, and I ran farther into the tent. I looked back. For some reason, two cages flanked the entrance of the tent, each containing a ferocious werewolf, their eyes as bright as torches.

Zara stood before me in gleaming silver armor, her black hair pulled back in a tight bun.

"Why the fook do you have caged weres at the entrance to your command tent?" I asked.

"I put them there to remind my troops what we're up against."

"Isn't that a bit dangerous?"

"It helps to weed out the idiots."

Zara led us to a large table covered with a huge map of the Red Garden. Figurines that represented the werewolves dotted the south with the fairies' positions marked in the north. From the looks of it, Oren Nero was right. Zara was winning the war.

Her hammer stood propped up against a filing cabinet, its head stained a dark red, no doubt from bashing in were skulls.

"A general, huh?" I asked.

"Still a detective?"

"Is this a competition?"

"Certainly not. It wouldn't seem fair. I have an army... and you have the skeleton of Madame de Pompadour?" She looked skeptically at Garry.

"Are you a general or an insult comic? His name is Garry, and for your information, this fella's been through a lot."

Garry made a sad face.

"Jack, I have a war to fight. Can you tell me why you're here?"

"I thought we were friends."

"Can you tell me why you're here, pal?"

"That's better." I held my arms out to the sides, smiling. "I think we all need to get along. Like a family."

"This is weird. You're acting weird." Zara raised her eyebrows. "Did you run out of dust? You usually call on friends when you need to get high?"

"I don't get high, first of all. I take fairy dust to control my cravings. It's medicine and in the public's interest. Is that how you think of me? A no-good dust head?"

"That's exactly how I think of you. No offense."

"Fair enough. I'll cut to the chase. We need your help."

"I'm busy. I don't have any interest in being part of your silly case."

"What makes you think I'm on a silly case?"

"You're always on a silly case."

"Is saving the world silly?"

She sighed. "Oh, that again?"

"I'm sorry that the world is in danger again, Zara. I don't want to inconvenience the great fairy general."

"As I recall, you didn't save anyone. You usually have other people do that for you. By the way, how is Oswald?"

I took the sleeping homunculus out of my satchel and held him up. "Alas, poor Oswald. I knew him well."

Zara grimaced. "That's kind of morbid, you know? Carrying him around like some rag doll."

"If you help us, we can save Oswald."

"I really don't have time for this, Jack. We have a large werewolf battalion trapped at the southern edge of the Bone Yard."

"If it wasn't for Oswald, there wouldn't be any Fairy Land, there wouldn't be any Pandemonium. I think you owe him a minute of your time."

"Okay, Jack. How are you going to save Oswald?"

"Show her the book, Garry."

Garry removed the journal from his pocket and handed it to Zara.

"What's this?" she asked.

"An alchemist's journal. He found Ratzinger's souls."

"Our souls," Garry said.

"Garry thinks the alchemist can also revive Oswald. It's the only chance we have. I've tried everything else."

"I still don't see why you need me," Zara said.

"Can you read the writing in the book?" I asked.

Zara gave it a look, flipped a few pages, and then closed it and handed it back to Garry. "I've never seen that language before."

"Precisely. The only guy who can read this book and help us find the alchemist is locked up on Purgatory Island. I need you to help us break him out. You won't be gone long."

She laughed. "Break out a criminal so he can read a book that may or may not lead you to an alchemist who may or may not be able to revive Oswald, who may or may not already be dead? Oswald was right about you and your plans. They're bad."

"Oswald liked you," I said.

"I feel terrible about Oswald. I really do. But you were the one who made him cover the Jupiter Stone. It was your plan."

"You won't help us?"

She shook her head. "No, Jack."

Zara was a stubborn witch. She couldn't be persuaded by sentiment. "Thank you for your time, general." I bowed graciously.

"You're just going to give up, Jack?" Garry asked. "What about our souls?"

"We'll just have to make due without them, Garry. We'll be fine. We're just a couple of stupid zombies, after all."

"Save me the sob story, Jack," Zara said.

"We did come all this way. Can we at least get some refreshments before we head back to save the world?"

"Then you'll leave?"

"Scouts honor."

"Devil Boy, I take it, and for the skeleton?"

"Milk, of course."

"Of course." Zara walked out.

I stepped over to her hammer.

"Jack, what are you doing?"

"Shut the fook up, Garry." I hefted the hammer. Boy, was it heavy. It took some doing, but I was able to stuff it inside my magic pocket. "Now, very calmly, let's walk out of here."

6

Hammer Time

WE CAUGHT A ride in the back of a wagon drawn by an old unicorn with a concave back. A bunch of fairies on shore leave headed back to the docks.

"Why did you steal the general's hammer?" Garry asked. "She doesn't look like the type of person who'll be happy when she finds out."

"No. She won't be. She's going to be furious. That's why we're going to say you stole it."

"Me? Are you joking?"

"Trust me. We'll tell her all about how your brain doesn't work so good. You picked it up thinking it was your walking cane or something. If that doesn't work, maybe she'll take it easy on you because of your skeleton pattern baldness."

"I don't like this."

"Get used to it. It's my style."

The unicorn followed a winding road through the grassland. It was quite beautiful in this part of the city. Butterflies and pixies flittered through the air, which smelled of fresh rain and strawberries. If not for the war, I could see myself retiring out here.

We boarded the turtle ferry just before the crew closed the gate. We sat in the back, and I watched the docks.

"I still don't see why you stole that hammer?" Garry said. "Can it help us break out Wally?"

"That's what I'm counting on."

The ferry horn blew. Right as the turtle's flippers began to move, shouting and banging erupted. Garry looked at me with an "oh fook" expression.

When that half-pixie, half-witch appeared on the docks, she was all witch. She bounded onto the ferry—hopping onto the turtle's tail in a giant leap.

Garry stood. I tugged on his arm. "Sit down. Let me handle this."

Zara raced up the tail, leaped onto the carapace, and rushed into the seating area. "You stole something from me." Her eyes hurled daggers.

"Not me," I said with my most innocent look. "Garry, do you have something to confess?"

"What's that, Jack?" he asked, his eyes darting back and forth.

"Garry's brain doesn't work so good on account of his missing soul," I said. "I have to apologize for him."

"Cut the crap," said Zara. "I know you took it, Jack."

"Do I look like a thief to you?"

"You look like someone who's about to have his head shoved up his arse."

"You're already on the boat, and it's already moving. We'll be back in no time."

"I already told you I'm not going on this crazy mission of yours."

"We need to find these souls before the Nazis get their hands on them. They're looking to assemble an army of the dead, which they're going to use to take over Pandemonium. It's a classic Nazi move. Me and Garry would rather not be a part of that psycho show."

She grabbed my shoulders. "I have my own worries with the weres in the Red Garden."

"Need I remind you that you'd still be locked up in the Duke's prison if Oswald hadn't broken you out."

"The Duke?" Garry said.

"Yeah, she used to date that nut. Can you believe it?"

Zara lifted me off the ground. "Remember when I kicked him over a mountain, Jack? Do you really want me to kill you too?" She shook me like a maraca.

"The Duke's not dead," Garry said.

She stopped shaking me, but still held my shoulders.

"Excuse me?" Zara squeezed me, hard. "How would you know that?"

Her fingers dug into my skin like needlepoints.

"The Nazis revived him," Garry said.

"Did you know about this?" Zara shifted her glare back to me.

"The first I'm hearing of it. Why didn't you say this before, Garry? By the way, you're hurting me, Zara."

She squeezed harder.

"I didn't think it was relevant," Garry said. "The Nazis do a lot of crazy things. They're Nazis!"

"Why would they resurrect the Duke?" Zara asked.

Garry scratched at his head, careful not to mess the dead thing on top of it. "I don't know. Maybe they like resurrecting people."

Her eyes narrowed. "Where is he?"

"He's at their compound on Witch End," said Garry.

Zara released me. My shoulders felt like they had been in a vice.

She sat, breathing heavy and staring straight ahead. I gave her some room.

"Give me the hammer," she said.

Zara looked incredulous as I pulled the hammer from my inside pocket.

"It's a magic pocket," I said.

"I figured. A pocket with a pocket universe. It's not as special as you think."

She removed the armor on her right arm, touched the weapon to her bicep, and the hammer changed back into a tattoo. Tattoos of all sorts of useful things covered Zara's arms. She could conjure any of them by uttering a few words and touching the ink. The hammer was her favorite.

"I'll go along with you two corpses, but then you're taking me to this Nazi compound so I can kill that piece of scum."

"Deal," I said. "I knew you would come around."

The witch clocked me in the jaw.

I fell straight on my arse.

No point in getting into a fight with Zara, so I let it slide.

"I guess I deserved that," I said, "but I'm not sure for what."

Zara shrugged. "Let's not talk for awhile. Okay?" I sat next to her. Garry took a seat across from us.

I ran a hand over Zara's armor. "It's so shiny." She slapped my hand. "I have so many questions."

"I've always wanted to ask you if you have bowel movements, but sometimes it's better to leave your curiosity to yourself. Didn't I tell you to be quiet?"

"You tell me a lot of things."

"You're an idiot, Jack."

"I find it to be my strength. Did you work your way up in the army, or did they just bestow a generalship on you once you whipped out your hammer? I never took you for the patriotic type."

"You know nothing about me."

"Dammit, Zara, won't you open up? Let me in. I want to know all about you. I thought you were going back to the Red Garden to reunite with your mother." I lit a Lucky Dragon.

"You want to know the truth?" she asked.

"Lay it on me."

"Give me a hellfire stick."

I pulled out another Lucky Dragon. She popped it in her mouth and I lit it.

She blew smoke in my face. "I joined the fairy army after I found out my mother was sleeping with the enemy and spilling secrets. She had disgraced my name. It was the least I could do. When I proved myself adept at killing weres, they promoted me."

"They trusted you even though your mother is a traitor?"

"They did after I killed her."

I blinked in shock. "You killed your own mother?"

"And her werewolf lover."

"Holy heck."

"I'm over it now. It's okay."

"When did this happen?"

"Two months ago."

I looked at Garry and grimaced. He shrugged.

"And when I kill the Duke—again—I can put my family issues behind me."

"The Duke killed her father," I said to Garry.

"He killed the wrong parent," Zara said. "This time, I'm going to make sure the Duke is dead."

"You don't have much luck with parents, do you? Your mother was a traitor and your father helped the Duke build the Pandemonium Device."

Zara walloped me again—with a haymaker to the jaw that flung me straight off the bench.

We sat in silence for the rest of the trip.

7

Hit the Fookin Devil Road, Jack

MY JAW STILL throbbed when we piled into the Studebaker, which I had parked by the dock in southern ShadowShade.

The pixie/witch made Garry ride in the back. He didn't argue. I doubted he could have taken a sock on the jaw. Most likely, he'd crumple into a pile of bones. I didn't argue either. I left Oswald in his satchel.

"Still not talking, Zara?" I started the Studebaker.

She didn't answer, the wheels in her devious mind turning. I could practically hear them churning. She was no doubt working out a plot to re-kill the Duke.

Zara and the Duke went way back. They dated for a time, until he murdered her father, a master sorcerer named Juan Carlos Villalobos del Toro. A good enough reason to end a relationship, in my opinion. Juan Carlos had recently finished making the Pandemonium Device when he got his pink slip in the form of a tombstone. I didn't like the idea of ol' Eddie McCrawley—his real name—being resurrected. He wasn't too pleasant before. The undead Duke wouldn't be an upgrade.

I took the Fookin Devil Road, also known as the FDR Drive, heading north. If I was lucky, traffic wouldn't be insane. If I was doubly lucky, the devil's minions wouldn't be out driving.

The Studebaker glided onto the entrance ramp. I wasn't lucky on the first count. Demon bikers, troll truckers, cryptid cabbies, psycho pedicabs—every alliterative automobiler you could imagine—shot down the narrow three-lane highway at breakneck speed.

I started to step on the gas, but jammed on the brake. "Missed it."

"Just merge, you sissy," Zara said. "You drive like a blind crone."

"Do you want to die before we even get to the other end of ShadowShade?" I stepped on the gas, but quickly hit the brake again. "Missed it."

Zara let out a sigh and stomped on my right foot. The Studebaker shot forward, heading straight for a semi with LUCIFER CORP emblazoned on its side. The driver blew his horn, an ear-shattering howl worthy of a banshee. I shut my eyes and pressed the gas pedal to the floor. We flew onto the FDR inches in front of the truck. The trucker gave me three more blasts of his horn and rode my arse.

"You're welcome," Zara said. "How about a little music? They're supposed to be playing a marathon of Kill Unicorn Kill tonight on K-HEL."

"Did I ever tell you the lead singer, Unicorn de Havilland, once hired me for a case?"

"That's gives you one point, brain licker. They're my all-time favorite band. It's a shame they broke up. Maybe you can introduce me to her when this is all over."

"She's not talking to me."

"When has that stopped you before?"

Zara turned on the radio with a blast of static. As she flipped through the channels, the static morphed into the chatter that rattled around in my head before the shadow men attacked us.

"Do you hear that?" I asked.

"What?" Zara had stopped on a station, but a thousand voices spoke in my head.

"Those voices?"

"You mean the Wolfman? Pandemonium's number-one DJ?"

The voices were barely whispers. I strained to make out the words. After a few seconds, it clicked—The voices repeated my name over and over.

jackjackjackjackjackjack

I turned off the radio.

"It stays on," Zara said, and reached for the button.

I swatted her hand away. "No! Leave it off!"

She must have heard the fear in my voice, because she left the dial alone. "Party pooper." She stared out the window.

"I need silence to think," I said, lamely trying to save some face.

High-rises flanked the road. This area had some of the best real estate in Pandemonium. Inside those luxury building lived the elite, the power brokers of the Five Cities, the bankers and politicians and moguls who sent you to Purgatory Island. I didn't know who had arranged for Wally to get pinched. Like me, the guy pissed off plenty of people, one of the reasons I liked him. Another reason: he was usually desperate enough to do whatever I needed.

Getting into prison, by definition, isn't difficult. I've spent some time on Purgatory Island myself. Each time on trumped-up charges—except that one time I stole Lucifer's goats. I didn't know he owned the goats when I stole them, and I might have been high on dust at the time, but I still got a thirty-day sentence. Though it was one of the worst months of my life, I did learn how to pick locks from a blind leprechaun.

The real problem with prison is getting out—which meant we would need to turn off the magic inhibitor. That shouldn't be a problem with Zara. She enjoyed destroying stuff.

The rest came to me in a flash.

My foolproof masterpiece of a plan went something like:

1) General Moonbeam marches me and Garry into the prison, pretending we're her prisoners. She hands us over to the dark elves.

2) Once we're inside, we find Wally.

3) Zara disarms or destroys the magic inhibitor. (Probably destroy.)

4) I use a bit of magic via The Book of Three Towers and transport the three of us out of the clink.

"So once again, I'm doing the dirty work," Zara said after I told her the plan.

"You're the one with the hammer," I said.

"Why don't you turn off the machine and I find Wally? I can do actual magic."

"Do you know what Wally looks like? Have you ever been a prisoner? Do you know the prison's layout?"

"Do you know where the magic inhibitor is?" asked Zara.

I shrugged. "How hard can it be to find?"

"I'm sure everything will work out perfectly. Are you even sure this wizard can help us?"

"He's Pandemonium's most extraordinary wizard," Garry said.

"According to whom?" Zara glanced back at him.

He pointed at me.

I watched a black Rolls Royce in the rearview, which had been there for most of our trip uptown.

"I think we're being followed," I said. "See that Rolls behind us?"

Garry and Zara both turned.

"How long has it been there?" Zara asked.

"For at least ten miles."

"Change lanes."

"In this traffic?"

"Don't be such a wimp."

I cut to the left, nearly colliding with a demon biker. The Rolls followed, bumping the demon biker into the guardrail. The bike and the demon both went over and fell out of sight.

"They're not being subtle about following us," Zara said.

"They're no longer following us. They're about to attack us." I sped up.

"Don't Lucifer's men drive black Rolls?" Garry asked.

"They do," I said.

"And why would they be after us?" Zara glared at me.

"That's a very good question."

"What did you two do?"

"Nothing. Well, nothing we're aware of."

"We were attacked by shadow men," Garry said.

"You failed to mention that back in Fairy Land."

"We didn't think it was important,' I said. "A day doesn't go by when I'm not attacked by something."

Another Rolls, twice as long as the Studebaker with black, impenetrable windows, pulled alongside us. It looked like a snake on wheels.

"Do shadow men drive?" I asked.

"Speed up," Zara said.

I hit the gas, but too late. The Rolls on our right swerved into us, clipping the back of the Studebaker. We fishtailed, but I managed to keep us on the road. I sped past the second Rolls. The first clung to my tail.

The second Rolls roared back up to my side. I swung the wheel hard to the right, slamming us into the demonic auto. It barely moved, but I was able to pull ahead.

"We have to get off the FDR." Zara rolled down her window. "Get us close to the Rolls."

No problem. The black luxury car had caught up to us, nipping at our tail. Zara pulled her bracer off, exposing some tattoos. She touched one by her left wrist, mumbled a few incoherent words, and a small cylindrical object appeared in her hand.

"What's that?" I asked.

"A grenade. You should go faster."

"You have grenades? Why haven't you used them before?"

"I like bashing shit better."

Zara tossed the bomb ahead of the Rolls. I floored it. The grenade exploded with an earth-shaking crack that hammered the back of the Studebaker. A brilliant flash of light and smoke swallowed the front end of the black car, while the rest of it slid into the stone barrier that ran along the edge of the right lane. Vehicles slammed into the luxury car from behind, causing a massive pileup. I flew down the FDR, weaving in and out of traffic. The other Rolls gave up chase, possibly to help its fallen comrade or because the driver didn't want to end up trapped in a pile of metal.

I took the 106th Street exit going eighty miles an hour.

The Purgatory Island Redemption

I DROVE NORTH on Third Avenue to avoid Lucifer Tower, which sat on 116th and Park Avenue.

"Anyone else after you two corpses?" Zara asked.

"I really can't say. I'm not very popular and neither is Garry. Right, Garry?"

"Absolutely. People usually despise me."

I pulled into an empty lot.

"We need to switch," I said. "Zara, you drive."

I got out of the car, put Oswald in the trunk, and hopped in the back seat with Garry. Zara got behind the wheel.

Garry said, "Shouldn't we be in handcuffs?"

"Where in the heck are we going to get handcuffs?" I asked. Then I remembered our tattooed lady.

"Which kind do you want?" she asked. "I have manacles, shackles, tethers."

"I'm not going to ask why you have so many tattoos of restraints," I said. "The plain old handcuffs will do."

Zara got out of the car, turned her back to us, and reached

into the front of her pants, touching the spot where she no doubt had a tattoo of handcuffs. The pixie/witch was full of surprises. A moment later, she pulled out the restraints and handed them to us. We slipped them on.

She got back in the car and drove us to a spot a couple of blocks from the ferry that would take us to the island. She used a glamour to hide the Studebaker, and hopefully keep any would-be thieves from taking off with Oswald.

Zara marched us to the 125th Street Pier.

No lights flickered on Purgatory Island, a dark hole in the middle of the sea across the black water.

The ferryman sat hunched on his skiff, smoking a hellfire stick. The dark elf's wizened face resembled an overused sphincter.

"I have two pieces of scum that need to be locked," Zara said.

The ferryman gave Garry and me the once over. "And what precinct are you with?"

"I'm General Zara Moonbeam of the Wee Free Folks Liberation Army."

"We don't get many generals around here. These two must be special scum."

"You have no idea."

We boarded the skiff, the ferryman gave his pole a mighty push, and we floated toward Purgatory Island.

The prison didn't come into view until we reached the shore. Dirt-streaked limestone walls, decorated with gargoyles and turrets and spires, surrounded the compound. Etched in stone above the entrance were the words: "Silence Is Golden."

The prison resembled a giant wheel with an octagonal hub at the center and seven single-story cellblocks radiating out from it. After landing on the island, a guard took us through the wall and into the eighth "spoke," a long corridor that led to the hub.

Nothing stirred as we made our way toward the center. The guard didn't speak to us. Somehow, even Garry remained quiet. We passed several locked doors. One had dark elves stationed on either side. I cleared my throat, hoping Zara would take notice. The guard shot me a dirty look.

A high stone desk dominated the hub, rising several feet above our heads, from which a dark elf looked down at us. Every part of his face was in the shape of a V. His bushy white eyebrows slanted toward his gray eyes and his pointy ears shot out like wings.

Zara didn't wait for the desk sergeant to speak. "Throw the book at these two pieces of scum."

The desk sergeant put a finger to his black lips. "Lower your voice, please," he whispered. "We don't want to disturb the inmates as they reflect on their transgressions."

"I guess not," said Zara in a hushed voice.

Dark elves stood at perfect attention at the entrances to each of the seven cellblocks. Other elves sat at lower desks working on silent typewriters or drinking coffee.

"Identify yourself."

"General Moonbeam of the Wee Free Folks Liberation Army," said Zara, "and these are my prisoners."

"We don't take political prisoners, and, pardon my bluntness, but you do not look wee to me."

Zara's eyes went wide. She leaned forward, an edge in her voice. "Is that a crack on my size?"

The desk sergeant again raised his fingers to his lips.

I stepped on Zara's toe. She needed to stay calm.

"Your massive size, do you mean?" the dark elf asked. "Next I expect you to claim you are a pixie." He laughed silently.

I couldn't do anything to stop it. Zara leaped over the towering desk and tackled the dark elf.

"Do you have a backup plan?" Garry whispered.

"I don't do backup plans," I said.

Zara and the dark elf tussled under the desk.

"Don't ever comment on my size or question my fairyness," she said.

Something thudded off the stone, most likely a dark elf skull.

Half of Purgatory Island's guards must have come rushing into the hub. As soon as Zara stood, they converged on her. She did pretty good for a while, flinging dark elves around the room like beanbags, but finally, they hit her with a stun gun and she went down.

"Lock that witch up!" the desk sergeant shouted. The elf bled from multiple places. He pointed at us. "I don't know what these two ghouls did and I don't care. Lock them up, too."

Two guards shoved us into a small room off the hub.

A bright yellow light burned in the room, empty except for a table between us and the two guards. One was short and squat with a brush haircut. The other was lean, tall, and bald.

"Strip," the bald one said.

"You mean take off our clothes?" Garry asked before turning to me and whispering, "You didn't say we'd have to get naked." His bones rattled.

"He's a bit shy," I said.

"I don't care what he is," Baldie said. "We have to check for contraband."

"He's a skeleton. It would be awfully hard to conceal anything on his person."

"Strip."

We got undressed, placing each item of clothing on the table. The guards groaned when I removed my drawers. They placed all of our clothes in bins, which they tagged and catalogued.

"We'll get them back when we get out, right?" I asked.

"If you ever get out."

Both guards laughed.

They didn't ask Garry to remove his wig. The dopes either thought it was his real hair or feared what they'd discover underneath it. The short guard ran his fingers through Garry's locks looking for contraband. Instead, he found a fat maggot. He gave a scream when it crawled onto his hand. After that, he left Garry alone. Perfect. Because I hid The Book of Three Towers under his giant bouffant wig.

"Let's just delouse these guys and call it a night," Shorty said.

"Make sure you get all the maggots, boys!" I said. "Watch that they don't bite."

"You two are disgusting, and we've had molemen in here."

They poured white dust from a cardboard box over us, got us good and covered like they were battering fried chicken. The powder tingled and burned. I guess that meant it worked.

They handed us prison uniforms, white pajamas with black stripes, and slippers.

"The prison's a bit crowded at the moment," the tall guard said. "So you two will have to bunk with someone else." The cells, as I recalled, were small, barely big enough to fit two prisoners. "But don't worry. Crawhook loves cellmates. We're pretty sure he ate his last two. We never did find a trace of them."

The guards led us back to the hub and then into the third corridor on the left. As we made our way down the granite stairs leading into the cellblock, a long, narrow hall with cells on either side, the whispers of inmates filled the air. Eyes appeared in tiny half-moon cutouts, the only openings in the wooden cell doors.

"I can smell 'em from here," a gruff voice said.

"A couple o' dead ones," another said.

"Was the cemetery full?"

Garry rattled and clanked. I put my hand on his shoulder.

The guards stopped before the second to last cell in the block. "Number fifteen!" he shouted.

The distinct click of a lock opening came from the door. Apparently, someone at the top of the corridor controlled the cell door locks. I made a mental note of that.

"In ya go," the dark elf said.

"Don't we get a trial?" Garry asked.

"You look guilty to me." And with that, the dark elf slammed the cell door.

Our cellmate, Crawhook, I assumed, looked huge, even lying down. His bare feet, bigger than ham hocks, dangled over the cot. His head—bald, lumpy, and scarred—sat like a boulder on a pile of pillows. He didn't look like an ogre or orc. He might have been a cross between a blob fish and a troglodyte. Beady eyes, full of loathing, peeked out of folds of droopy flesh.

Garry said, "I guess we should make the best of this." He stuck out his hand. "How do you do, I'm Garry. This is—"

"Where's yer meat?" Crawhook asked.

"—my pal Dead Jack."

I wondered where they put Zara, and if she had a bunkmate. Attacking the desk sergeant had been a pretty stupid move on her part. She was probably spending too much time with me.

"Garry's a skeleton," I said.

"Did someone eat him? What kind of meat was on you, bones?" Crawhook's right hand balled into a fist and rested on the stone floor.

"What kind?" asked Garry.

"Was it savory, salty, fatty, lean?"

"I'd like to think I was sweet."

"Ever taste yerself?"

"Can't ever recall."

Crawhook shifted his attention to me. "What about you, ugly?"

"What are we talking about here?" I asked.

"Regular prison talk, pally. Just a couple of inmates chewing the fat." Crawhook laughed. He sounded like a man dying of lung disease.

"Sounds sexual to me."

"Does it now? Nothing sexual about eating another creature's meat. It's survival. Do you like to cuddle after you take down a juicy meat bag?"

"See, that sounds sexual."

"You're screwy. Listen to my pal Johnny. We've double-teamed on eating plenty of creatures together." Crawhook knocked on the wall to his left. "He's a werewolf. Johnny, is there anything sexual about eating some guy's meat?"

After a long silence, Johnny said, "I'm not speaking to you."

"Don't be that way, you hairy beast." Crawhook gestured with his thumb at the wall. "He's just mad because—why are you mad at me, Johnny?"

"You know why. Now go and play with your new friends."

"Oh, I see," Crawhook said. "He's jealous." He shouted, "These guys don't mean anything to me! I'll show you!"

Like a cobra, Crawhook sprang from the cot and gazed covetously at Garry's bones. He stood at least seven feet. "I could make a nice shank with the collar bone and that skull would be a boffo mug. Strip! I want to see the rest of your bones."

"Are you serious?" Johnny growled from the other cell.

"This is all getting a bit too out of hand," I said.

"I wasn't talking to you, corpse blocker." Crawhook yanked Garry's prison shirt off. The skeleton reflexively covered his breast bones.

"Garry's spoken for," I said.

"Is that so?" Crawhook pushed Garry aside and stood before me. I nearly fell back from the stench, a mix of beef stew and dirty feet. "What are you going to do about it?"

He jabbed me in the chest, shoving me back against the cell door.

"This isn't my first time in lockup, pally," I said.

"So we've got ourselves a repeat offender."

"You don't want to mess with me."

That hoarse dying man laugh again. "Did you eat your pal's flesh? I bet you did."

I ran a finger over Crawhook's bicep. It was like iron. Then I put the finger to my lips. "I've eaten my fair share of Pandemoniums."

"Eat this!" Crawhook fed me a knuckle sandwich. I cushioned the blow with my teeth. My head slammed into the door and it swung open. I fell on my arse outside the cell, just as all the other cell doors began to open.

A tall human ran from door to door waving his finger at the locks and shouting, "Open sesame!"

The prisoners rushed out of their cells and swarmed to the hub.

The lunatics had gotten loose in the asylum.

"Zara!" Garry shouted. "She must have destroyed the magic inhibitor." That wasn't part of the plan, but neither was Zara getting arrested.

Garry tried to push past Crawhook, but he blocked him with an arm.

"You two ain't going nowhere."

"You're free to go, dunzy," I said after getting to my feet. "What're waiting for?"

"Why would I leave? I have my heart's desire right here."

"Again, that sounds very sexual to me."

Crawhook bounded out of the cell, grabbed me by the throat, and lifted me. I tried kicking him, but I was like a baby trying to swim away from a shark. The bastard spit out a thick green tongue and licked me from forehead to chin. "Smokey."

"You're giving off a real creepy vibe," I said.

Garry emerged into the hall clutching his breastbone, as Johnny came tearing out of his cell. The werewolf's ribs pushed out of his flesh. Bite marks covered his body. Looks like Crawhook had been chowing on his next-door neighbor. Johnny leaped in, clamping down on the creep's throat with his slavering jaws, knocking him to the ground. The werewolf ripped and tore out the creature's neck.

"We're not friends, by the way," Johnny said. "Just so you guys know, Crawhook was kind of an asshole."

Dead Jack and the Soul Catcher

"We'll take your word for it." I took off down the corridor, Garry close behind. "I need the book."

"Right. Sorry." The skeleton gently lifted his toupee and slid The Book of Three Towers out before handing it to me.

"There's a locating spell in here that'll bring us to Wally."

I flipped to a section conveniently called LOCATION SPELLS and read the spell to myself.

"Why aren't you reciting a spell?" Garry asked when we got to the end of the cellblock.

"There's a problem. I need a map of the prison for it to work."

"You didn't check the spell before we got locked up?"

"I'm winging it, Garry."

We entered the hub. It was empty, but a commotion came from the end of the main corridor, the one leading to the outside world. A klaxon sounded. Silence, apparently, was no longer golden.

"How are we going to find Wally?" Garry asked.

"Easy." I ran around the hub, shouting, "Wally! Wally! Wally! Wally!"

"I don't know why I didn't think of that."

"That's why I have the detective license and you don't." I poked my head into the second corridor and shouted Wally's name. No answer. A fire engulfed the third block.

"What if he's with the others trying to escape?" Garry asked.

"Then we may be out of luck."

I stuck my head in the fourth corridor and shouted, "Wally! Wally! Wally! Wally!"

"Be quiet," a voice said.

"Wally, is that you? Come on, Garry."

We raced down the stairs and entered the cellblock. All the doors were open, except one.

Why hadn't he taken off like the others?

I opened the door.

Wally stood in the middle of the cell, his back toward us. The cell was twice the size of the others and filled with the comforts of outside life: a couch, bed, lamp, rug, wireless radio, and bookshelves. "For chrissakes, that was terrible," he whispered.

Wally is a korrigan, a cross between a gremlin and a fairy. He stood barely up to my waist, his hands on his hips, his long brown ears drooping to his shoulders.

I was about to say something when it became apparent he wasn't talking to us.

Admission time about Wallflower. He's not the most reliable wizard in Pandemonium. Truthfully, he's not even a good wizard. In fact, he's pretty much a disaster as a wizard. More of a mountebank. A charlatan. A fraud, really. He makes bogus amulets and elixirs of life. Cons dragons out of their treasure hoards. Why do I rely on him? Wally adores me and he is quite brilliant, if he's mostly a scam. And he really is a whiz at languages.

"Do you sincerely believe you can win the competition with such a deplorable performance?" Wally asked the air.

"Hey, Wally, it's your old pal Jack. I'm here to bust you out."

He still didn't turn, but continued to talk to someone or something that apparently wasn't in the room.

"You said you've been practicing, that you had it down," Wally said. "Didn't I say the competition would be fierce this year? The wendigo in cell block five has the voice of an angel."

"Wally, who are you talking to?" I asked.

The wizard slowly turned and looked at me without expression. "You're late."

Before he had gotten pinched, Wally had been a heavy-set little guy with an enormous potbelly. Now he didn't have much more fat than Garry. His head, though, having remained the same size, looked way too big for his tiny, frail body.

"Did we walk in on something here, Wally?" I asked.

Wally's eyebrows wiggled. "What's your talent?"

"I can't die."

"That won't do. Are you a song and dance man? I can really use one."

"Wally, stop messing around. We disabled the magic inhibitor. We're breaking you out of here. We need you."

"I'm not going anywhere until we finish the talent show. They try to break you in here, but we won't let them. Right, Lucius?" Wally turned to his left and looked up.

An awkward silence hung between us.

"We've been practicing for weeks," he continued. "At least I have. I'm not sure about Lucius. He keeps getting his steps wrong. It's a one-two-three. Shimmy-shimmy." Wally did what can best be described as a jig.

Great, the wizard was bonkers. He must have been kept in solitary a bit too long.

"We win the talent show every year," he said, "and I'm sure not going to change that. So if you can't help, stay out of the way, ghoul. Your friend, by the way, is naked. This is a family-friendly show. Please, tell him to cover up."

"This is your brilliant wizard?" Garry asked.

"He's eccentric," I said. "Give me a minute. Can I audition, Wally?"

"Do you have any talent?"

"Loads. I'm going to read a dramatic monologue, if that's all right."

"Wonderful."

I opened The Book of Three Towers.

I didn't feel very confident after the locating spell. Maybe transportation spells are easier. I hadn't used that one too often—meaning never. What could go wrong?

I said the words, twirled my fingers, and—poof!—we vanished.

Funny thing about spells: They need to be done exactly right to work properly. Every "t" needs to be dotted, every "i" needs to be crossed. Apparently, I had forgotten to cross one of those i's, because we landed in the middle of the warden's office. In fact, we landed on top of the warden. From the sharp crack, I figure at least two of his ribs shattered. Believe me, I know the sound of ribs shattering. This might have been a problem, but when I stood, it became apparent the warden had already died, as had several of his guards.

"What the heck happened here?" Garry asked.

The dark elves' bodies lay scattered around the room. One sprawled over the desk, another's head had gone through a file cabinet. Green blood splatter covered the walls and the door had been smashed to crap.

"Zara happened," I said.

"What are we doing here?" Wally asked.

"The talent show has been canceled, Wally," I said. "On account of the prison going to shit."

"Darn, darn, darn. We had been practicing for months."

"Wally, we have a much better show, bigger stars, bigger audience, for you to join. Come with us."

Zara ran into the room, panting, and threw two bundles at us—our clothes. "Get dressed. I do not need to see that." She pointed at Garry's naked body. We scooped up the clothes.

"Turn around," I said while pulling off my prison garb. Zara did.

"What the holy heck happened?" I asked.

She patted her hammer. "Revenge."

It felt good slipping my fedora back on. Garry was back in his awful zoot suit.

"Are you with us, Wally?" I asked.

All hell had broken loose outside. Inmates stampeded past the office, shouting and howling in elation.

"If there's no talent show, there's really nothing holding me here. Lucius?" Wally tilted his head as if listening to someone. "He says he likes the skeleton's wig."

"Is that a yes?" I asked. Wally shrugged. "Good enough."

We headed out of the warden's office into a smoke-filled hub. Up ahead, a tremendous crash announced the prison's front doors opening. Sounds like it's time to get the fook out of here.

Between the Devil and the Broken Sea

"SO THAT WENT smoothly," Zara said when we reached the Studebaker. Patches of dried blood coated her cheeks and forehead. A bruise darkened under her right eye.

I didn't know if she had gotten injured when she battled the dark elves or when she tried to save the ferryman from the fleeing prisoners. They ended up tossing him into the Broken Sea anyway. We commandeered the ferry after Zara ripped off an escapee's nose and shoved it down his throat. Several of the inmates ran back to their cells. The others let us be on our way.

I worried the glamour hadn't worked and Upper East Side thieves had gotten into the Studebaker. With a hand wave, Zara brought back the invisible car. I opened the trunk, my heart pounding. When I found Oswald still in his satchel next to the alchemist's journal, I finally relaxed.

I slipped the satchel over my shoulder. "All in all, it went better than most of my missions. No one died."

"No one except the warden, all his guards, and several prisoners," Garry said.

"No one who mattered."

"We can't stand around here too long," Zara said. "Where are we going?"

"That depends on what Wally finds in the journal."

"I hope he's as good as you say he is," she said.

I swallowed hard. "He won't disappoint us. Right, Wally?"

"We need to get back to the prison," Wally said. "The talent show is tonight."

"Wally, there's not going to be a talent show, remember? The prison was overrun." He stared at me. "We need you to translate a journal."

"Oh, I stopped doing that years ago. There's no money in it."

"It's very important that you help us. A lot is riding on it."

"A lot is riding on the talent show. Lucius and I have been practicing for weeks."

"Lucius?" Zara asked.

"He's Wally's special friend," I said.

Zara scrunched up her face as if to say, huh?

I held up a hand. "Don't ask."

"You said this was the guy." Zara pointed at him. "You said he was a great wizard."

"He's just a little off on account of his prison stay. He'll be right as rain soon enough. Do you need a little dust, Wally? A little of the sparkly stuff?"

"Did you know Lucifer puts the ground-up bones of the dead in fairy dust? I have documents. Proof!"

"Is that a yes or no?"

"Stimulants don't interest me. Dulls the third eye." He tapped the middle of his heavily furrowed forehead.

"Stop wasting time," Zara said. "Give him the journal."

I handed Wally the journal. He took it and gazed at the front cover for a long while, turning it over in his hands as if he had never seen a book before. I was about to tell him that you need to open a book to read it, but he finally cracked it open.

"We don't know the language it's written in," I said. "We need to know where the person who wrote the journal is located. We're hoping the book will give us a clue."

He gave the opening page a glance and handed it back to me. "I can't translate it."

Zara and Garry stared at me.

"I thought you knew every magical language in existence," I said.

Zara and Garry kept glaring at me.

"It's not written in a magical language," Wally said. "It's in code."

"Can you decipher it?"

"Sure." Wally snapped the book shut.

"Great."

"It will take me no longer than seven days."

"We don't have seven days. We have a few minutes at best."

"Then you're out of luck. Can I go back to jail now?"

"Look, you don't have to decipher the entire thing. We only need to find where the alchemist is keeping our souls."

I flipped to the images of the soul vessels and showed them to the wizard. His eyes widened.

"Souls," he said, in a creepy voice. "I've always wanted

to get my hands on some souls. I can get a pretty penny for them, you know? There once was an alchemist who was buying them up for big bucks a few years back."

"Are you fookin kidding, Wally?"

"I think his name was Alberic. Boy, did he love to journal."

My hands shook from excitement. "Wally, I think this is our guy."

"He was always going on about how difficult his lair—that's what he called it—how difficult his lair was to find."

"Wally, do you know where it is? Did you ever go there?"

"No, it was a secret lair in the Dire Wood. I would never go there."

"The Dire Wood! Perfect!"

"Sorry, but I can't help with the book. I'm terrible at cryptography."

"Wally, I knew you could do it."

Wally turned to Garry. "Is this zombie nuts?"

"Come on—let's get in the Studebaker before something bad happens," I said.

"Too late." Garry pointed over my shoulder.

Shadows came up from the earth and dripped off the trees. They fell from the sky. They pooled on the ground. One by one, they rose into vague man-shapes, tall and thin as reeds.

Shadow men surrounded us.

The wind whistled and howled as a black car sped around a corner and came screaming down the road.

I flicked my lighter on and held it up. A gust blew it out.

"I don't think that's going to work here," Garry said.

Zara conjured her hammer.

The car stopped, the door opened, and out slid a red-faced

demon in a three-piece suit. Two sharpened horns jutted from the top of his head. He looked like the sort of accountant who'd have no problem helping you cheat on your taxes.

"That was quite the scene you all caused on Purgatory Island," he said with a mocking bow.

I figured if I could make it to the Studebaker and throw on the headlights, I could take care of the shadow men. The demon would be another story.

"You broke about a dozen laws and are harboring a fugitive," the well-dressed demon said, his face shiny and slick. "But we're not concerned about all that."

"And by we, do you mean Lucifer?" I asked.

"The Man has requested your presence at Lucifer Corp."

The shadows glided toward us.

"We're not going anywhere." I flicked on my lighter again and cupped it with my other hand to protect it from the wind.

"He only wants to discuss a business proposition. No tricks. He's the good guy here. If you don't want the deal, you're free to go."

"Those shadow men tried to abduct Oswald."

"Let's talk at the tower. We have refreshments." The demon flashed a slimy smile.

"We'll meet you there," I said.

"No. I'm afraid I'll have to take you." The demon took a step forward.

"Come any closer and the witch will bash in your skull."

The demon held out his hands. "You can trust me."

A screech came from the sky.

I looked up. At least a dozen long, emaciated beasts flew overhead, their ribs showing through their dull gray skin.

DEAD JACK AND THE SOUL CATCHER

The soul suckers, their beaks like curved ice picks, dove. But they were the least of our worries. Riding the creatures were Nazis, but not any Nazis. These fookers had been dead a good long time.

I was wondering when those bastards would show up. Certainly word had gotten out about our prison break.

The demon shouted to his shadow men. The shades rose to twice their size.

When the soul suckers neared the ground, the undead Nazis leaped off their mounts.

Zara attacked before their boots even touched pavement, knocking Nazis back into the sky with mighty swings of her hammer. I caught a wing in the face and went down. As I scrambled onto my arse, I glimpsed a Nazi woman with blonde hair and blue eyes wearing a little black cap at a rakish angle. The only live human in the group, she stayed atop her soul sucker. She winked at me and circled the fray like a Valkyrie waiting to escort the dead to Valhalla.

The soul suckers hung back, screeching like dying krakens. Shadow men engulfed the zombies. Soul suckers inhaled shadow men. A Nazi zombie came lumbering through the fray directly at me. He smiled, exposing bleeding gums. He had muscles on muscles. His Nazi uniform stretched so tight over his body I expected buttons to shoot off like bullets at any second. I hated zombies. But I hated Nazi zombies more. I put up my dukes as Garry rattled like a pair of castanets. Wally watched it all like a spectator at Ebbets Field.

The big zombie kept coming, pushing other zombies out of the way. He launched a haymaker from the back of his ear. I sidestepped, but his knuckles still managed to brush the side of my head. It stung good and I fell into the posh demon's arms. He dragged me off as a group of shadow men descended on the giant zombie.

The demon let me go when we reached safety. It looked like the shadow men had the upper hand—until the Nazi blonde yelled, calling in a second battalion of winged zombie demons from high in the sky. They looked like the infernal creatures that had died atop Monster Island during the battle over the Pandemonium Device. Ratzinger must have sucked up their souls and now used the beasts in his army.

The Brooks Brothers demon said, "You need to come with me now or we're all food."

Finding myself stuck between the undead and Lucifer, I figured Lucifer was probably our best bet.

"What kind of refreshments do you have?" I asked.

10

AN OFFER YOU CAN REFUSE

"WELCOME TO LUCIFER CORP.," a disembodied female voice said as we entered the tower's lobby, "a shining light in the darkest of places. No refunds, no returns."

Lucifer Tower is the tallest and most famous of Pandemonium's three towers, 102 stories of gleaming steel and glass. While the Bone Tower and Obsidian Tower are shrouded in mystery and supposedly unoccupied, Lucifer Tower doubles as the headquarters of the Lord of Hell's business operations. Besides Devil Boy and Lucky Dragon, Lucifer manufactures a line of unicorn steaks and his own strain of fairy dust (which I had never tried due to its exorbitant price). He owned casinos in ShadowShade and Witch End, and Pandemonium's only five-star hotel. He was the Boss of Bosses and generally kept Pandemonium's most powerful gangs from each other's throats.

We rode an elevator with the well-dressed demon, who had introduced himself as Eric Allen.

"Here at Lucifer Corp., we care about one thing only," Eric said. "Profits."

"Just like every other corporation," I shot back.

"Yes, but unlike every other corporation, we don't pretend to care about our customers or employees."

"Well, that's refreshing," Zara said.

The elevator came to a stop, the doors slid open, and the stench of brimstone hit us.

"You should air this place out." I waved the air in front of my nose as we stepped off the elevator.

It looked like any other corporate office, everything made of shiny, smooth wood—the floors, the walls, the chairs, the desks. Giant murals of the war between good and bad angels in heaven surrounded the reception area. Lucifer, of course, led the bad angels.

The receptionist, an ancient, shriveled demon in red lipstick, said, "He's expecting you."

We crossed the room and entered Lucifer's office. More of the same Art Deco crap here, the 1930s version of luxury and modernity. Lucifer stood from behind a lacquer desk almost as wide as the office. He wore a pink golf shirt and duffer cap. I didn't even know Pandemonium had a golf course. Above him hung a painting of a winged angel plummeting from heaven. He barely resembled the painting. In person, Lucifer was much less majestic.

"What a beautiful crew you are." Lucifer smiled. He looked mostly human, though his skin had the dusty red of bricks, and the lines of his face ran too well defined—chiseled and sharp. "I don't mean that aesthetically. Because some of you are downright gruesome. I'll let you figure out who, but I'm sure you already know. I say 'beautiful' because you are the promise of this heavenly hell. Where else could you see a zombie, a skeleton, a korrigan, and a witch/pixie banding together? It's a fookin melting pot, Pandemonium is. A paradise. One I don't intend to lose."

"We were promised refreshments," I said.

"Of course, Jack! A man worthy of my own appetites. Get the dick some Devil Boy. The good shit. Not the watered-down crap we sell to the public. You like dust? I have a new strain. Third Circle. I think you're going to like it. Can I get anyone else anything?"

"They're good," I said. "We'd like to hear your offer, so we can get out of here."

He nodded at his henchman Eric, who then left the office.

"Take my card, Jack. If you ever need dust, give me a call." Lucifer snapped his fingers and a business card appeared in his hand, which he offered to me. I slipped it in my front pocket without giving it a glance.

Eric returned with a pint of Devil Boy in a glass bottle and a baggie of bright yellow dust on a silver tray.

I took the Devil Boy and put the dust away. I sipped the formaldehyde, a burn of golden fire slid down my throat.

"Good stuff." I held up the bottle to Lucifer.

"You know quality, Jack. Wait till you try the dust. It's going to blow your mind. I'm expanding my business. We're going to have flavored hellfire sticks—apple, cinnamon, blood, kraken—injectable fairy dust, a franchise of pleasure palaces. It's going to be the bee's knees."

"Just more ways to sin," Zara said.

"No. There is no sin in Pandemonium. 'Do what thou wilt' is the law of the land. Wallflower knows what I'm talking about."

Wally lowered his head.

"And what does that have to do with us?" I asked. "Did you bring us here to pitch a new line of unicorn steaks?"

"I want to maintain the status quo. I have big plans for Pandemonium, and I don't want those wet blanket Children of Thule putting the kibosh on them. Garry's fun-hating pals want to make Pandemonium like the Other World. They want to bring sin into our world. That's not going to happen in our little Garden of Eden. Not while I'm around."

"I still don't see what that has to do with us."

"Do you know what you have in your purse, Jack?"

"It's a satchel." I laid my hand over the bag. "And he's just a lump of rubber."

Lucifer shook his head. "No. No. No. Don't be a fookin idiot. If he was just a lump of rubber, why would you be carrying him around everywhere you go? Why would you protect that lump of rubber with your life?"

"Habit."

Lucifer laughed. "To be honest, I'm happy you have such strong feelings for the homunculus. Otherwise, he may have fallen into the wrong hands, and that would be valde malus."

"Why would that be?" Zara said.

"Because your friend is walking around with an A-bomb in his...satchel?" Lucifer said. "Actually that's not accurate. It's more like a thousand A-bombs. After your little battle on Skull Mountain, that lump of rubber is now a living, breathing Jupiter Stone. You didn't destroy it. You can't destroy it. That homunculus of yours absorbed its power. He's a remarkable creature. You should have been nicer to him."

I looked at Zara. She looked at me. We didn't know what

happened to the Jupiter Stone, to be honest, and if Oswald really is indestructible, maybe he did absorb the stone's power. It would explain why he felt heavier.

"The only thing I want to do is remove the stone and give you back your friend," Lucifer said. "If you don't separate him from it, he's never going to wake up. And sooner or later, you're going to blow up Pandemonium and everyone in it."

"Would that be so bad?" I asked.

"I'll have to keep my eye on you, Jack. You have a dark soul. Oh, wait, I forgot. You don't have a soul."

"Got any spare souls?"

"Looking to make a deal? Let me fix up Oswald and I'll give you the best one I have."

"And you get the Jupiter Stone? For what?"

"I've always wanted one of my very own. I've heard they can come in handy."

"I'm supposed to trust Lucifer? You don't have the best reputation."

"Don't believe the newspapers. If the Nazis get their hands on Oswald, your life and everyone else's is going to be much worse."

"Worse than you ruling it?"

"Rule it?" He laughed, a bit more maniacally than I cared for. "Why would I want to do that? There's no fun in ruling. Too much responsibility. I prefer chaos. Shit blowing up. People freaking out. Every day you don't know what to expect. It's called Pandemonium for a reason. Those damn Nazis want to rule it. They want to drain all the color out of this place. So boring. I want to keep Pandemonium true to its name. Danger around every corner and dust in everyone's pocket."

"What makes you think they're even after Oswald?"

"I heard a rumor—maybe Garry can back me up here—but I heard they want to use the Jupiter Stone inside Oswald to power a soul sucker, who will then suck up all the souls on Pandemonium, even the living ones."

"Garry?" I said.

The skeleton stared at the floor. "Well, actually, I heard that they were trying to increase the soul suckers' power, but they were never able to do it. I never heard them talk about Oswald or a Jupiter Stone."

"Could Oswald power a soul sucker?" I asked Lucifer.

"I think Oswald could do just about anything he wanted," he said.

"Except wake up."

"Why don't you just go and wipe out the Nazis yourself?" Zara asked. "You don't need Oswald or a Jupiter Stone."

"The bastards have drawn an impenetrable magical circle around their camp. No demon or shadow man can get inside. They're not pushovers. They have a lot of power, and they're coming for you. When we remove the Jupiter Stone from Oswald, the Nazis will have no reason to bother with you four. You'll be safe."

"I still don't like it," Zara said. "If you remove the stone, Oswald could die."

"He's already dead," Lucifer said.

I'd heard all I needed to hear. "I respectfully decline your offer," I said. "I'll keep the dust, though."

"Are you sure?"

"Sure as hell."

Lucifer dropped down on his leather office chair. He adjusted his cap, and let out a sigh. "I'm sorry to hear that,

Jack. I really am. You might not believe it, but I am a man of my word. And as I promised, you're free to leave."

We didn't move.

"Go," Lucifer said. "I'm already late for my golf game."

The well-dressed demon led us back to the elevator.

We got in. He did not. When the doors closed, I said, "Maybe I had Lucifer wrong. I didn't think he'd ever let us go."

"Get your head out of your arse," Zara said. "He's not going to let us go." She already had her hammer in her hand.

11

Take This Job and Shove It

THE ELEVATOR DESCENDED faster than Lucifer from God's grace. I held on to the wall to keep from falling. Screams or the sound of machinery came from passing floors. Strange lights glowed on the other side of the door.

"Is it just me, or is this speeding elevator taking a really long time to get to the lobby?" Garry asked.

"I don't think we're going to the lobby," said Zara.

"More like the Ninth Circle of Lucifer Corp.," Wally said.

"We must be halfway to the Other World by now," Garry said. "Maybe the elevator is broken."

"No," Zara said. "Lucifer has plans for us."

The elevator screeched to a stop and we all took a tumble.

"Jack, I had no idea the detecting business was so dangerous," Garry said as he used my body to pull himself up.

"I haven't noticed," I said.

Zara tried hitting the buttons, but the elevator didn't move.

"I think we're stuck," Garry said.

Ding!

The elevator doors slid open. A stench worse than the swamps of the Red Garden hit us, a smell full of damp and vapors. An animal smell, like the reptile house at the zoo.

The light from the elevator illuminated a small patch of dirt-covered ground beyond the door. It was quiet, except for the sound of dripping water in the distance.

"Are we just going to stand here?" Garry asked.

At that moment, something long and black shot out of the dark. An arm, a tentacle, a whip. I had no idea. It extended into the elevator, thin and hairy, wrapped itself around Garry, and yanked him into the blackness. It happened so fast he didn't even scream.

"To answer Garry's question," I said, "I don't think we should just stand here."

"After you, corpse," Zara said.

"Despite what some may say, I am a gentleman." I extended my arm. "Ladies first."

"How sweet. A gentleman and a coward."

"Since I know you're joking, I'll take that in the spirit in which it was meant."

Zara stepped onto the dirt. She looked left and then right. "I can't see anything, but, boy, does it stink."

"I have a lighter," I said, "but, Wally, do you have anything better?"

The wizard cupped his hands and twisted them in opposite directions. A glowing orb appeared between his palms, the light bathing his leathery face in pale blue. I followed him out of the elevator.

The stench worsened out here. It burned my nostrils and watered my eyes. The air hung over my face like a warm, damp rag.

"I think I found something." Zara bent down and held up a bone. "Do you think it's Garry's?"

I took the bone, possibly an ulna, held it up to my nostrils. "Smells like fresh milk. It's Garry all right."

"I guess we're going in the right direction."

I put the bone in my satchel.

We crept forward. Vague shapes appeared in the distance—jagged, sharp forms, possibly stone. We stuck to a narrow rut, but numerous passageways snaked off into the distance.

"Do you think we're still in the tower?" Wally asked.

"No," I said. "I think we're deep underneath it."

I almost tripped over Garry's foot. "Found another one," I said, and picked up the bones.

"I think we've been left a trail," Zara said.

"Is Garry really that important?" Wally asked.

I thought about it.

"Isn't he your friend?" Zara said.

"He's more of an acquaintance, a former co-worker. We haven't been in touch for a while. It's not like we exchange Christmas cards."

"Keep moving."

Tik-tik-tik. Something chirped, most likely the large, horrible monster that lived under Lucifer Tower. The sound bounced off the rock formations, making it impossible to locate its source.

Wally held up his orb of lighting.

I looked in all directions, but didn't see a thing move.

The chirping faded, and we continued on, more cautiously.

I found Garry's other foot.

We crested a hill and found a wide clearing below.

Torches bathed the area in an orange-red glow. As we crept down the slope, I noticed a skull sitting atop a pile of bones at the far end of a large pit. A disheveled wig sat atop the skull.

"How does my hair look? I can't fix it."

"Who did this to you, Garry?" I asked.

"I couldn't see. It was dark. But whatever it was it stunk."

Tik-tik-tik.

The sound grew stronger.

Zara, Wally and me stood back to back to back, searching the sunken chamber.

Tik-tik-tik.

A sound like the creaking of leather and the whooshing of silk surrounded us.

Tik-tik-tik.

An enormous spider emerged from the shadows directly above Garry. Eight red eyes flickered open. Its slime-covered fangs clicked together, making that tik-tik-tik sound.

We all backed up to the other end of the pit.

The creature eased its considerable bulk to the ground. Furry, many-jointed legs moved in absolute silence as it padded toward us.

Zara held up her hammer, Wally held up his orb, and I fixed my fedora.

The spider stopped in the middle of the pit, its bloated underbelly resting on the ground.

"Hi," I said. "How are you?"

Three ropes of silk shot out of from the beast's spinnerets, each of which wrapped around our bodies. In a flash, the arachnid had us strung up like sides of beef in a meat locker.

"He wants me to eat you," the spider hissed in a voice

like boiling water. "Suck up your flesh and toss your rotten bones in the heap. He tosses all his garbage down here for good old Syd to take care of. Did you trust the Devil?"

"A devil," I said.

"Pardon?"

"He's not the Devil, just a devil, lowercase. Technically, there are three Dukes of Hell—Satan, Lucifer, and Beelzebub."

"I didn't know I had an expert demonologist in my midst." The spider raised its two front legs and brought them together in a slow clap.

"It's pretty common knowledge."

"Is it? Then you'd know that Satan, Lucifer, and Beelzebub are actually three aspects of the same being, collectively known as the Devil, a sort of Unholy Trinity of God."

"Are you saying they're the same person?"

The giant spider let out a sigh, like he had to explain this many times before. "They are three persons in one being."

"Like a hydra?"

"If the hydra's heads were separate entities."

"That makes no sense at all."

"Think of it like this: The Devil is one, undivided 'thing' but three 'people.' Or, they are not each other. They are all the Devil."

"So there are three Devils?"

"No. There is only one Devil, uppercase."

"You're making my head hurt. If there's only one Devil, why aren't Satan and Beelzebub here in Pandemonium?"

"You'd have to ask him that."

"All I know is that they're all rotten."

"Tell me, then, if you're such an expert on demons, how did you end up in Syd's lair?"

"I admit mistakes were made."

The spider laughed, a chittering laugh. I had never made a spider laugh before, so I felt a sense of pride.

"I too have made mistakes. Boy, have I screwed the pooch. My mother always told me not to rush into things. You get hired at Lucifer Corp., you think you're set for life. You have a career, not just a job. I've given Lucifer Corp. the best years of my life and what do I have to show for it? I thought I'd work my way to the top, but fifty years later, and I'm still in the sub-sub-sub-sub-basement. Where's the opportunity? The upward mobility?"

"Stuck in a dead-end job?" Zara asked.

"Lucifer Corp. is a shite hole. What do you think I got for my fiftieth anniversary? That's a lot of beings eaten."

"A watch?" I said.

"A watch? I would have cherished a watch. No. I got a spittoon. Not even a nice one."

"Do you spit a lot?"

"I do now. At least get some use out of the fookin thing. But what should I expect from that slimy bastard upstairs? Oh, he took on God and the Archangel Michael. Big deal. They tossed him from heaven like a snot rag. I asked for an espresso machine. I heard they have three of them upstairs for the 'executives'"—he made air quotes with two of his legs. "I've been eating his enemies for five decades. And believe me, they don't taste like coq au vin. He says it's not in the budget. Budget? The piece of shite owns Pandemonium. Five grams of dust would pay for the espresso machine." The spider let out a sigh, shook its oblong head, and continued its rant. "Do you see that mold buildup?" The spider pointed at one of the black pipes that crisscrossed the ceiling. Fat drops of water fell from the shiny surface. "That's not there for some scary atmosphere. That's an actual leak coming from upstairs. Do you know how many times I've requested repairs?"

"One hundred times," I said.

"Don't get crazy. Twenty-five times. That's more than enough."

"You should go into business for yourself. Freelance. I'm sure there's plenty of work in Pandemonium for a giant spider with your experience."

"Don't think I haven't given that some thought. I'm crazy to stay here. I've tried before to escape, but there's magic blocking the way."

"There's a way out?" Zara asked.

"I found it in one of the tunnels, a pair of doors, but there's no way to open them. When I tried to break it down, Lucifer found out and cut off one of my legs." The spider raised its shortened rearmost left leg.

"You're in luck, pally," I said.

"You have a spare spider leg on you? I would give anything to have my leg back."

"No, we're experts in magic."

The spider rolled all eight of his eyes. "Like you're an expert in demonology? Geez."

"Zara here is a witch and Wally is Pandemonium's finest wizard."

"Did all the other wizards in Pandemonium die?"

"He's the best. Trust me."

"And what are you?"

"Dead Jack, zombie P.I."

"Pandemonium has really gone to piss, it seems. Maybe I should stay here."

"Pandemonium is the same shithole it's ever been, but

it's a thousand times better than this place. Take us to the doors. If we can open them, you can start a new life. Find opportunity, your true calling. The career of your dreams. If we can't, eat us. What do you have to lose?"

"Another leg."

"You have like ten."

"Spiders have eight legs, you fookin idiot."

"I know a great place for espresso in Downtown ShadowShade."

The spider gave it a moment of thought. "If you don't open the doors, I will devour each of you slowly, a strip of flesh a year."

Syd used his fangs to cut away my bindings.

"You're doing the right thing," I said.

After the spider freed me, it went to work on Zara and Wally.

"What about me?" Garry asked.

"We're not going to have time to put you back together," I said, while collecting Garry's bones.

"I can't stay like this."

I wrapped the bones in Garry's empty zoot suit, placed his head on top of the suit, and held him against my chest.

"Just don't mess up my hair, Jack. The dampness is destroying the texture."

Syd let out a loud whistle. As it faded, another sound—like the tik-tik-tik but magnified a thousand fold—echoed throughout the underground level. The pit filled with thousands of tiny shadows. The little patches of black flittered up from the rocks and poured out of the walls and ceiling. They gathered at our feet.

I looked down. There had to be at least ten thousand regular-sized spiders in the pit.

"I can't leave behind my children," Syd said.

"You're a woman?" I asked. I didn't have to wonder what's creepier—one giant spider or a thousand baby spiders—because I was facing both. Lucky me.

"Sydney Spinhook's my full name."

"Are we finally leaving?" the baby spiders asked in unison. It sounded like a swarm of locusts.

"Yes, children," Syd said. "You have Uncle Jack to thank."

The baby spiders turned to me. "Uncle Jack," they hissed, and ran up my legs and onto my chest and arms. "Uncle Jack! Thank you!"

I screamed.

"Come on, the tunnel isn't far." Syd climbed out of the pit and scuttled into one of the many passageways carved through the stone. Wally crept behind the spider, holding up his blue orb. Behind him, strode Zara, her head turning from side to side as if she expected an attack. At the rear, I shambled along.

The air grew warmer and dryer as we descended the narrow passageway. The baby spiders streamed like a black river over our feet. I didn't feel like tearing off my skin at all. When the tunnel widened, I walked alongside Zara. She raised an eyebrow and rubbed her tattooed arms. I knew what she was thinking. What if we couldn't open the door? We'd have to fight that thing and all her children.

Syd stopped, and a second later, light from Wally's blue orb fell on a wall of obsidian.

"Where are the doors?" I asked. The smooth-as-glass wall had neither a crack nor a crevice. Our reflections stared back at us in the highly polished surface.

Syd ran a hairy leg over the middle of the wall. At first,

only thin spider web cracks bubbled up inside the obsidian, shining like silken threads in sunlight, but gradually, they expanded and deepened, until a doorframe became evident. Words, too, appeared, delicate figures written in that same angelic language I first saw at the Duke's Broken Palace. Enochian.

"Can you read it?" I asked Wally.

The wizard stepped closer to the wall and held up his orb. "At the top are numbers—234—and under that it says, 'Only the keepers of knowledge may enter.'"

"What's that mean?"

"I think this is an Angel Gate. They can take you wherever you want to go. I had never seen one before. I thought they were only legend."

"How do we get in?"

"A magic word, perhaps?"

I glanced at Wally. "Do you know the word?"

The wizard held out his arms and, in a firm voice, said, "234."

Nothing happened. The spider sniggered. "Is he serious? Two hundred and thirty-four? Why would they put the secret magic word right on the damn door? I think we'll be feasting on wizard pretty soon, kids."

The baby spiders shouted in joy.

"Give him a chance," I said.

Wally shouted, "Open!" When the doors didn't open, he exclaimed, "Rood nepo!"

"You just said open door backwards! Come on with this guy!" The spider tapped her legs on the ground, impatiently.

"You'd be surprised how often that works," Wally said defensively. The wizard shouted words in every language he knew. Then he whispered them. Nothing happened.

He tried spells, he knocked on the doors, he tossed a few plasma orbs at it. For good measure, he even kicked it. Wally stood back from the wall, looked up to his right, and muttered something. Then he watched the wall for an awkward moment. "Lucius is having no luck either."

He sat on a rock, dejected.

Syd crept toward the wizard, salivating.

"Not so fast!" I said. "We haven't tried everything. Zara?"

The witch lifted her hammer and swung mightily at the doors. *Bwong*! It rang off the obsidian like it had struck a great bell. The force knocked her several feet back. The wall wasn't even scratched.

"I tried the hard way," she said, "Now I'll try the more cunning way." Zara stood before the doors. With her right forefinger, she traced figures in the air as she muttered a magical language that sounded like something between a whisper and a lullaby. But the doors remained closed. The pixie/witch tried other spells and mutterings. She tried other tattoos, including the grenade, and even the ol' kick, but nothing worked.

Saliva dripped from Syd's fangs in thick ropes. Her body heaved. "I had great hopes in you three."

"Do we have to eat Uncle Jack?" the baby spiders asked.

"I'm afraid so, kids," Syd said. "It's not like he's really your uncle."

I was hoping the spider kids would put up a fight, but they gleefully shouted, and streamed toward me.

"Wait!" Garry said. "Jack, don't you have The Book of Three Towers? Surely there's something in it that can help us here."

"The Book of Three Towers has nothing about the three towers in it," I said. "It's a bit of a false advertisement."

"There has to be something," Wally said. "You must not be reading it correctly."

"Oh? I think I know how to read, Wally. I'm pretty smart for a zombie."

"May I see it?"

"I'm not comfortable handing over my book."

Wally folded his arms. "Well then, I suppose we could have the spiders eat us."

"Don't crease the spine and if you dog-ear any pages I'll kick you in the throat."

I removed the book from my inside pocket, and noticed it had become thicker than usual, at least twice its normal size. I wondered if it had gotten wet and then I remembered the dampness. Had it become water-logged? You can never fix a wet book. I prayed it wasn't damaged. I flipped through its pages. It had changed. The script was different—smaller and more ornamental. Gone were the usual spells and rituals. I flipped to the table of contents.

I couldn't believe it.

It read:

A Brief History of the Three Towers
The East Tower
The West Tower
The North Tower
End Note

"What is it?" Wally asked.

"The book has changed. There's stuff in here about the towers, but they have different names."

"LST," Wally said, matter of factly.

"What?"

"Location-specific textuality. The content changes according to where you are. Apparently, you need to be inside or near the towers to access information about the towers."

"Why would the names be different in the book?"

"The towers were here before us," Wally said. "We gave them their current names. These may be their true names."

"So, how are we supposed to know which tower this is?"

"Give me the book, please."

I handed Wally the book.

He took and leafed through it until something caught his attention. The wizard stopped, read for a moment, then looked up at me. "Just as I thought."

"What?"

"It tells you right here how to access the door. On page 234." He gave Syd a triumphant nod. "Now stand back."

Wally recited from The Book of Three Towers: "East, West, North." With his right index finger, he traced the shape of a triangle, which—now that I thought about it—was the position of the three towers. "Through and through and through, open all the doors."

The door glowed white, then vanished, exposing a swirling vortex like a bowl of stars being stirred by a maniac god.

"We're just supposed to walk through that?" I asked.

"Only if you want to get stuck in oblivion," Wally said. "According to the book, you need to think of where you want to go as you enter. Otherwise you could wind up in limbo or some random place."

"Syd, where do you want to go?"

"What's the address of that espresso shop?" asked the spider.

The sound of running hooves echoed down the tunnel.

"Something's coming," Zara said.

"No doubt it's Lucifer's men," Syd said.

"Let's go! Think Bleek Street and caffeine," I said to Syd.

The great spider waved her children through the gate. "You heard Uncle Jack! Think Bleek Street and caffeine."

The baby spiders flooded into the vortex, as the demons drew closer. War cries emanated from the darkness.

"I can already smell the coffee." Syd dove through the Angel Gate and the swirling stars swallowed her.

"It probably wasn't a good thing that we let those spiders escape," Garry said.

"You all ready to jump to the Dire Wood?" I asked.

"Should we bother?" Zara asked. "The Nazis are after Oswald. They're probably not looking for the souls anymore. We should get him to a secure location."

The rasp of the demons' breath grew louder as they closed in on us.

"Reviving Oswald is the best chance we have of keeping him safe and keeping all our souls safe. Besides, we need to leave now."

We held hands and entered the Angel Gate.

Wally said, "Close," and the portal shut behind us.

I thought of dark and scary trees as I stepped into the swirling vortex.

12
A Not-So-Secret Lair

TIME FROZE INSIDE the vortex. Though I had seen a bright white light as I entered, once inside, it was pitch-black—no sounds, no sights. I tried calling out to the others, but if I made a noise, I didn't know. I was alone, walking, I thought, but I couldn't feel my feet land on the ground. I caught my mind wandering and pulled it back to the Dire Wood. I had never been there before. Witch End is a place I avoid, since it's mostly inhabited by humans, and humans hate zombies more than anything in Pandemonium.

The Dire Wood is situated in the Northwestern corner of Witch End, known in the Other World as Queens. From what I know of the wood, it's a wild area full of ghosts and wolves. It's famous for the number of suicides that take place there. Most people go there specifically to off themselves. But others, it is said, are driven to it once they step within the wood.

I daydreamed of hanged corpses swaying from trees like

piñatas when I suddenly realized I was walking in the real Dire Wood. I hadn't noticed any change or transition. I just went from imagining the Dire Wood to being there. I looked up. Only two corpses in the trees—a human witch dressed in a wedding gown and an elf in a tuxedo. The perfect metaphor for marriage.

"That was weird," a voice said.

I screamed, and Garry's head went tumbling to the ground. I had forgotten all about him. His head rolled until it smacked against a crumbling tree stump. I ran over to him. His face was stuck in the dirt. I picked him up and dusted him off as best I could.

"How's my hair?" he asked. "Is it on straight?"

"How can I tell?"

Zara appeared ahead of us, looking around, seemingly in a daze.

"Zara, over here!" I shouted.

She turned toward me and headed in our direction.

When she reached us, she asked, "Where's Wally?"

I looked in every direction, but couldn't find the wizard.

"Do you think he messed up?" I asked.

"And didn't think of the Dire Wood?"

"He might not have wanted to go with us," Garry said. "He seemed to like being in prison."

"That dirty stinking jail bird!" I said.

Someone screamed.

"Lucius! Where are you, Lucius!"

"It's coming from there." I pointed toward the south.

We caught up with Wally, who was stalking through the wood like a blind man who had lost his cane.

"How can you lose an imaginary friend?" I asked.

Wally didn't like that. He stared daggers at me. "Lucius

is not imaginary, you rancid piece of meat! He's just as real as you."

"Maybe he thought of a better place to transport himself to."

The wizard's face darkened. "He went back to prison! To perform in the talent show! He had his heart set on it. I have to go back."

"Wally, we're in Witch End. You have no way to get back. Not to mention, we have important business here."

"That's your business, not mine. Lucius!"

A wolf bayed.

"It's probably not a good idea to be shouting like that, Wally. Let's find the alchemist's lab and then you can go back to prison if you want."

The korrigan's face wrinkled. He seemed to think about it. "Lucius does need more time to practice. Still, we need to hurry back."

"Trust me. I don't want to stay here any longer than is needed."

"Hey, can you reassemble me while we're at it?" Garry asked. "I need to scratch my nose."

I dumped Garry's bones onto the ground and placed his head at the top.

As I searched for Garry's spine, I said, "Any idea where the secret lab is, Wally?"

"None."

A warm breeze blasted through the dead trees. Their naked branches shook nervously.

"Maybe it has something to do with the fact that it's secret?" Zara asked.

I found the spinal column and tried to snap it into Garry's head, but it wasn't happening. I held the spine firmly with one hand, placed Garry's head over it, and slammed my fist on top of his noggin. That did the trick. It clicked into place.

"Careful with the elf hair!" he said.

"So how are we going to find the lab?" I asked.

"I'll ask a snake," Wally said. "They know hidden things."

I attached Garry's rib cage, and his arms. I left the rest up to him.

Wally got on his hands and knees. He dug a hole in the ground, bent over it, and whispered strange words into the earth.

The wind howled and the trees creaked like secret doors in haunted houses. The sky was the color of a fresh bruise.

Movement stirred in the browned grass.

Wally patted the dirt next to the hole, first softly, then violently, and a long, jade-green snake slithered toward him.

The snake stopped inches from the wizard. He got up on his knees. The snake rose, too, half of its body pointing straight up. Wally spoke more strange words. It sounded like he tried to spit but couldn't muster up any saliva. The snake watched the sorcerer making noises like a flat tire expelling air.

When he stopped, the snake flicked its tongue several times. Wally bent closer to the creature, putting his ear to the snake's mouth. I couldn't make out what it said.

Wally jumped up. "I most certainly will not!" he shouted. He turned to us "What a disrespectful snake. I take back everything good I've ever said about snakes. Apparently, they are not such upstanding creatures."

"What did he say?" I asked.

"She wants me to provide a service for her in exchange for the information."

"What does she want you to do?"

"She says there's something stuck in her throat and asked if I could get it out."

"What's wrong with that?"

"She says the only way I can remove the obstruction is with my tongue."

"The poor thing is probably suffocating. Don't be so selfish, Wallflower. Pretend it's Lucius."

"I'll pretend you didn't say that."

"We're wasting time," Garry said. He was back together and in his atrocious zoot suit. "How's my hair look?"

The snake, her eyes watering, held herself straight up and waited for Wally to save her. She coughed. Wally leaned in, stuck out his tongue, and inserted the long brown thing into the serpent's mouth.

"Root around in there," I said, "and find that damn obstruction. We don't want a dead snake on our hands."

Wally probed the snake deeper and deeper, the reptile fluttering the end of her tail. When he couldn't go any deeper, the snake jerked her head back, then darted into the wizard's mouth. The slimy thing had gotten almost halfway down his throat before he managed to pull her out with a popping sound. The snake dropped to the ground. I thought I saw her smile.

Wally spit and wiped his mouth. "I can't believe I fell for that."

The snake turned, hissed, and slithered off. Wally, still wiping his mouth with the back of his hand, followed. "Come on. She's taking us to the lab."

The snake led us through an overgrown area of the wood. Thick, muscular brambles covered the ground and wrapped around fallen trees. My feet kept getting tangled up in the weeds, their razor-sharp thorns slicing at my ankles.

The snake deftly navigated the treacherous terrain, which soon cleared to a glade. A few rotten tree stumps and boulders sat in the grass.

The snake entered the glade and then took off like a shot, disappearing into the wood.

"Great," I said. "That snake was a real snake. We got duped."

My head filled with the static again. But this time a single voice rose above the hissing with more clarity. Faint and far away, it whispered something about the boulders, but I couldn't make out the rest.

Three boulders lay scattered across the glade.

I had the faint idea the voice belonged to Oswald. But it couldn't have been. He hadn't spoken since we destroyed the Pandemonium Device. I lifted him out of my satchel. Still lifeless, just a ball of fluff. Was I losing it imagining the runt's voice? Before he fell into a coma, he never stopped talking. He sure did his best to drive me crazy then.

Still, I walked over to the boulder at the far edge of the clearing. It was about six feet long and three feet high. I placed my hands on it and the thought of pushing it entered my mind. So, I did. At first, it didn't want to budge, but I put a bit more muscle into it and the rock gave a little. Zara joined me and pushed, too.

The boulder slid backward, exposing a wooden trapdoor.

"What made you push that boulder?" Zara asked.

"Would you believe deductive reasoning?" I said.

"Not at all."

I really had no idea why I pushed it. Maybe I was developing extrasensory perception.

I gave the trapdoor a tug, but it was locked pretty tight.

"Maybe we should knock," Garry said. I looked at him. "After all, this is private property. Alberic might not be very happy if we just go barging inside uninvited."

"He has a point," Wally said. "There's also a good chance the door is enchanted to ward off intruders."

I tapped on the trapdoor. "Hello, down there. Anyone home?" I waited for an answer, but didn't get one.

"What if he doesn't want to let us in?" Garry asked.

"Why are we arguing about this?" I asked. "We have hammer girl over here and a world-class wizard. Let's bash down the door and figure it out later."

"That's your plan?" Zara said.

"Do you have a better one?"

"Hammering things usually is my plan. I just wanted to make sure."

I stepped aside. "Bash it to fookin bits."

Zara swung her hammer with two hands like a carnival strongman. The door splintered into dozens of pieces.

"So much for an enchantment," I said. "Who wants to be the first in the hole?"

We all looked at each other. Then, with reluctant bravery, Garry said, "I started this. I'll go."

Wally conjured his blue orb of lighting and held it over the hole. A makeshift ladder of wooden planks ran down one side of the shaft. We couldn't see the bottom.

"Tell us right off if there are any monsters or maniacs down there," I said.

"Should I use a code word or something?" Garry asked.

"Say, 'Oh, fook, there's a monster down here.'"

"Sure, buddy, sure."

I slapped him on the back, and then Garry gently lowered himself into the shaft.

"Your hair is looking great, by the way," I said.

Garry didn't respond. He descended into the darkness. In a moment, he'd disappeared from sight. "It smells terrible down here." A few seconds later, he gave out a yell and a dull thump echoed up from the hole.

After an awkward moment of silence, he shouted, "I think my right foot fell off!"

From the sound of his voice, I estimated he had fallen only about twenty feet.

"Any monsters, Garry!" I shouted.

"I can't see, buddy!"

"I'd go next, but, Wally, you have the light."

The wizard gave me an incredulous look. I shrugged. Wally entered the hole. I followed and Zara came down last.

We stood in a small antechamber that barely fit the four of us.

Wally's orb of lighting lit a narrow passageway on the far end of the antechamber.

"Lead the way, Wally," I said.

We crept into the passage one by one, and stepped out into a long hall that went off a long way toward the left and right. The walls were made of dried mud, like a house of adobe.

"I think we're in a labyrinth," Wally said.

"This guy really didn't want to be found," Garry said.

"If this alchemist is as paranoid about being discovered as I think he is, we could be lost in here for years," I said. "Any ideas?"

Again the brain static, the mind radio searching for a

station. A voice whispered, louder. This time, I could clearly make out its words.

Go left.

"Oswald," I asked, "is that you?"

"What?" Zara said.

I froze like I had been caught with a worm coming out of my nose. "I thought I heard something."

"Keep it together. Okay?"

"Follow me," I said, and took the lead.

As we delved deeper into the labyrinth, I thought about Oswald. Did he tell me to push that boulder? How did he know what he knew? How was he communicating with me? It wouldn't be the first time Oswald took up residence in my head. That's how we met. The little fook spent six months inside my skull. He said he was just looking for a place to sleep. I never believed that.

The smell of earth and rot grew stronger the farther we walked.

"What if this alchemist doesn't want to give up the souls?" Zara asked.

"That's a great question," I said, and left it at that.

The voice, welling up in my mind like bubbles in carbonated water, continued to guide me.

Make a right…continue on straight here…stay to the left.

It sure sounded like that annoying pipsqueak voice of Oswald's. He somehow beamed himself directly into my noggin. Was he talking telepathically to me? No one else could hear him. I tried to talk back in my mind. Is that you, Oswald? Are you waking up? You're sure taking your sweet time. I got no answer.

"Isn't there usually a monster in the middle of a labyrinth?" Garry asked.

"You're thinking of the Minotaur," Wally said.

Garry turned his skull toward Wally with a faint creak. "Wasn't he a monster?"

"One of the worst."

"Don't put ideas in his toupéed head," I said.

"He brought it up."

"Stop!"

Wally held his hands up in surrender. "I didn't say anything!"

"Look. Up there." I pointed at a dark form in the middle of the path.

We stared at it for several minutes.

"It's not moving," Zara finally said.

"Maybe it's sleeping," I said. "Minotaurs sleep, don't they?"

"Then this would be the perfect time to fight it." Zara gave me a shove.

I stumbled a step but caught myself. "Who said anything about fighting it?"

"You could try befriending him, spend some quality time with the Minotaur, share your life stories, bond, and then when he's your best buddy, you cut his throat."

"Wouldn't work. People generally don't like me."

"True. Then a fight to the death it is. Good luck."

I conjured up all the brave I could and crept toward the form. Is it a Minotaur? I asked Oswald in my mind. No answer.

As I got closer, I could make out a foot. What did a Minotaur foot look like? Did he have a hoof? No, he was a man from the neck down. The thing on the ground looked human. I grew braver and crept closer. A grayish robe with many tears and holes, like rats had been at it, covered the rest of the body. The corpse lay on its back, its shriveled and leathery face staring at the dirt ceiling with eyeless sockets. The front of the robe, right by the heart, had been slashed and bore dark stains. Ancient blood?

"I think I found Alberic," I shouted back to the others.

They crammed around me and looked down at the body.

"That's why there was no enchantment on the door," Wally said. "Any of his security measures would have died with him."

Garry must have followed my line of thinking, because he backed away, shaking his head. "I couldn't have known, Jack. I'm sorry."

"So much for him helping us revive Oswald," I said, and wanted to strangle the skeleton.

"There are still the souls," he said, in a quaking voice.

"Who gives a flipping fook about the souls!"

"I do. They're our souls, and without our souls, we are nothing but an assemblage of bones and muscles—sometimes even less—that only knows hunger and despair. Souls are the breath of God. You can't throw that away, buddy."

"Spare me the Goddy bullshit, Garry. I have an idea. Alberic may be of some use, after all."

I knelt beside the alchemist and took out my stash of fairy dust. He may have been dead too long, but it was worth a shot.

I licked two of my fingers, dipped them into the baggie, and then wiped the dust on the alchemist's desiccated lips.

"What are you doing?" Garry asked.

"The dust loosens the lips of the dead."

Several minutes passed, but the corpse didn't speak. I dabbed my fingers in more dust and coated the alchemist's black tongue. The dust crackled and snapped like ice melting on a fire.

"What happened to you?" I asked the corpse.

Silence.

"How did you die?"

A long release of air emanated from the dead alchemist's throat.

"How did you die?"

A voice of gravel and fire spoke. "Al…ra…un," it said.

I asked the corpse more questions. Where he kept the souls? Who was Alraun? But I got no answers.

When I stood, the others gave me queer looks.

"Did you hear what he said?" I asked.

But they shook their heads. "He didn't say anything," Zara said.

"What do you mean? He said Al-ra-un."

"You said it."

"What do you mean?"

"First, you let out this long breath and then you said 'Al-ra-un' in this really weird voice."

"It was creepy," Garry said.

That had never happened before and I had used that dust trick on quite a few dead people.

"Let's keep moving," I said.

I no longer needed the voice to guide me through the labyrinth. Somehow, I knew where to go—right to the center of the labyrinth.

"Any of you know what Alraun means?" I asked.

"It's the German word for mandrake," Wally said.

"Do you think he meant a mandrake killed him?"

"Maybe. Mandrakes are known for killing whoever digs them up."

"We should be on the lookout for mandrakes," Garry said.

"The alchemist has been dead for decades," I said. "If that mandrake knew any better, he'd have left this dump long ago."

After a few more twists and turns, we reached the center of the labyrinth and the alchemist's lab. The doors hung open.

"How did you know your way through the labyrinth?" Zara asked. "And don't tell me deductive reasoning, because you don't do reasoning."

"I'm a good detective, Zara. Why can't you just accept that? While you take the blunt way, I take the meditative, delicate way."

"Something's going on here."

We entered the lab. Wally's orb cast a blue pallor over the place. The books outnumbered the equipment. Fat, leather-bound tomes and papers covered every surface. Beakers, tubes, and cauldrons of all shapes sat on a long table in the center of the room. Against a wall sat a surgical table, thankfully without a corpse on it. To the right, a desk covered with more books and papers.

Garry found some candles, and we lit them.

Wally sat at the ancient desk, blew dust off a pile a papers, and began to read. I investigated the table in the middle of the room. Zara watched the door as Garry wandered around in search of the souls. I didn't think it would be that easy.

On the table, I found three tall glass jars containing little dolls. A black one, a blue one, and a red one. They reminded me of Oswald, but these figures were misshapen and featureless. Then again, Oswald didn't have eyes until

I etched X's into his big head. The dolls sat limp inside the jars. I tapped the glass and waited anxiously for a reaction. They didn't move. I lifted the black one out of the jar. Its skin had the same texture as Oswald's. A gelatinous blob. They lay there just as dead as Oswald. I didn't want to think what this could mean. But I couldn't ignore the implications. Were these Oswald's brothers? Were they, too, murdered like the alchemist? Or had they never been given life? For all I knew, every alchemist had these homunculi in their labs. I didn't know what an alchemist did. I had only heard rumors about philosopher stones, but I knew they had nothing to do with philosophy. As I've often said, Oswald is an enigma wrapped inside a marshmallow. Given how much time we spent together, I knew little about him and his origin. I didn't even know for sure if he was a homunculus.

"I think I found something!" Wally shouted.

We all rushed over to the desk where the wizard sat.

"Did you find the souls?" Garry asked.

"Something better. Alberic's writings." Wally held up a sheaf of yellowed paper.

"What was he working on?" I asked, wondering if the document contained anything about the homunculi and Oswald.

"All sorts of things. He really was a genius. A shame he was killed."

"Quit stalling," Zara said. "We need to get out of here as soon as possible. I don't like the idea of being trapped in this burrow."

"The souls aren't here," Wally said.

"Then let's get out of here." Zara stepped toward the doors.

"How do you know?" Garry's voice went high.

"Keep your wig on and listen to this." Wally read from the diary:

Bad, evil dreams again last night. Every night since I found the vessels. I must move the souls out of the burrow tomorrow or something terrible will happen. They have power. And nothing must stop me now. I am so close.

"At least that confirms he had the souls," Garry said. "I told you, Jack."

"He doesn't have anything," I barked. "One, he's dead, and two, the souls aren't here."

"But they have to be close by. He wouldn't put them too far out of his reach."

"He's probably right," Wally said.

Boom-doom, boom-doom.

The sound echoed from deep within the labyrinth.

At that moment, I realized Zara had been right. Being in a burrow spelled trouble.

The sound of stomping boots thundered in our ears.

"Trouble's coming." Zara pulled the doors closed.

"It might not be a great idea to cut off our only exit," I said.

Zara found a lead pipe and used it to bar the doors. "It's a worse idea to leave the doors open, don't you think?"

"Nazis or demons?" I asked.

"Or demon Nazis or Nazi demons," Zara said. "What difference does it make?"

My mind radio turned up to maximum, crackling like a bonfire.

jackjackjackjackjackjack

My dead skin prickled.

"Oswald?" I asked.

"No, my name is Zara. We've gone over this."
"Sorry."
"Focus."
"Wally, can you magic us out of here?"
"I can try. Gather in a circle."

We did, holding each others' hand. Wally closed his eyes and mumbled under his breath, before saying, "Something's binding me. There's someone out there with strong magic."

"Garry, look around for another exit," I said.

The skeleton nodded and headed into the shadows.

Boom-doom, boom-doom. The sound rattled throughout the labyrinth, and blended with the voice in my head, which continued calling my name.

jackjackjackjackjackjackjackjack

Something big lumbered up to the doors.

We looked at each other, holding our breath. A soft rapping preceded a soft, feminine voice.

"Hallo." The playful tone startled me. "I didn't have a chance to introduce myself at the pier before you all took off so suddenly."

The Nazi woman who led the soul suckers?

"I don't want to call you guys out, but it did seem a bit rude. I have to admit my feelings were hurt. But that's in the past. Let's start over. My name is Dr. Ilsa Hellstrom."

"How did they follow us here?" Zara asked.

I gave Garry a dirty look. He shook his head and backed away.

"Let me tell you why I'm here and we can go from there," said Dr. Hellstrom. "Okay? I work for some very important and powerful people and they have tasked me with retrieving the homunculus/Jupiter Stone hybrid. We feel it is very important to our current plans. I have been given carte blanche when it comes to obtaining the creature, which I believe you call Oswald. He sounds like a real cutey. In short, what I am trying to say is open the doors and hand over Oswald or I and these very scary zombies are going to kill all of you, or at the very least torture you until you wish you were dead. Okay? I have said all I've needed to say. Your response?"

"No thanks," I said.

"I can't very well go back to my superiors without the homunculus. How would that look for my career trajectory? And my employee review is coming up. So, you can see the quandary I'm in. Can you help a working gal out?"

"Sorry. We don't help Nazis."

"Technically, it would be neo-Nazis. But they don't like us using the N-word too much. We're advocates for Pandemonium's human population. So, you can call us 'humanists.'"

"No, I'll call you Nazis. It's easier to remember."

"Is that you, Jack? I've heard so much about you from Ratzinger. He really misses you, you know? He feels like you're a son to him." My skin crawled. "Oh, Jack, dear, do me a favor and open the doors before my men break them down. I'd hate to see them dirty their uniforms. It would get me really steamed. They're such smart-looking outfits. You're going to flip when you see them in good lighting. We can fix you up in nice duds, too. Were you buried in that suit you're wearing?"

Nazis. Fookin crazy Nazis and their uniforms. I could hear it in her cocky, psychotic voice too. "I'd rather go naked."

She laughed, a sharp, biting laugh like a wolf baying. If

I had blood in my veins, it would have drained out of my body.

Garry returned, out of breath. He whispered, "There's a back door, Jack, but it's blocked."

"Show me."

Wally and Zara followed us to the back of the lab, mostly, a storage area with more books, boxes, and beakers.

"Here," Garry said, and stopped. A large wooden chest sat in front of the door.

"I tried to reason with you," Ilsa said. "Knock the fookin door off its hinges and then bash these badly dressed losers." Something crashed against the front doors—a Nazi zombie, no doubt.

Me and Zara got on one end of the chest and pushed. Damn it was heavy. When we got it out of the way, I grabbed the knob and yanked. It came off in my hand. Another crash rattled the front doors.

Boom-Boom-Boom. The front doors sounded like they'd give out soon, the hinges cracking and bending.

"Move out of the way," Zara said.

The second I stepped to the side, her hammer came whistling through the air and blew apart the door. We ran back into the labyrinth. Without warning, my satchel felt heavy and weighed down, like I was carrying a dozen bricks.

jackjackjackjackjackjackjackjack

The voice practically shouted.

I took the lead and we ran around the outer perimeter of the lab until we came to a passage.

Was the runt finally coming out of his coma? I lifted him out of my satchel. He must have quadrupled in weight. I needed both hands to hold him up. His weight wasn't the only thing different about him. He throbbed like a beating heart and glowed so brightly it burned my eyes.

jackjackjackjackjackjackjackjack

"Are you waking up or about to explode?" I asked. I remembered Lucifer's words: You're carrying around an A-bomb, Jack.

I'm fine, Oswald said, loud and clear inside my head. I had known, on some level, that the static came from him, but not until that moment did I admit it. He had been warning me, guiding me this whole time.

We turned right and plunged down another corridor. I instinctually knew the path. Did I know because he knew?

The banging from the Nazis faded off to silence. Not even footsteps chased us. I wasn't stupid enough to think they had given up.

Oswald, how do you know what you know? I asked in my mind. You weren't so bright when you were alive.

I'm still alive.

Then wake up. I'm tired of carrying you around. If this was all a scam to get me to lug you everywhere, I'm going to be pissed.

I'm not ready to wake up.

Fookin prima donna.

We made another right, and Oswald glowed brighter. I had to close my eyes. When I opened them, we stood face to face with the Nazi fooks.

Zara pressed next to me. Garry and Wally held back.

"Hi, Garry." Ilsa Hellstrom waved. She wore a cheery smile, exposing ivory white teeth. "Your hair looks like shit, by the way. You really need a new wig."

Garry harrumphed.

"You told them we were here, Garry?" I demanded. "You traitorous bag of bones!"

"Not me, buddy! I swear."

"If you idiots don't want your secrets out, you shouldn't talk to snakes," Ilsa said.

She wore the same black mirror-shiny jackboots and form-fitting black slacks as the undead soldiers. Her shirt, however, was a crisp white topped with a short red tie. Her hair had been pulled into a tight ponytail and a little black hat sat atop her head, askew. Half a dozen zombies in—I had to admit—boss uniforms stood behind her. All black. Well-tailored. White piping. High stiff collars with lightning bolts in red. Caps too. Next to Ilsa stood the biggest, baddest zombie I had ever seen: an undead Goliath with a face only a Nazi could love. Half of it had been obliterated. Exposed muscles bulged from his neck.

The Nazis had taken me by such surprise that I had forgotten I held Oswald.

The zombie King Kong made a beeline for me. I tried shoving Oswald back in my satchel, but I was too slow. The undead beast drove his shoulder into my stomach, slamming me against the wall. Oswald went flying. The glowing white ball dropped right into the Nazi bitch's hands.

"That was much easier than I thought it would be," she said, and chuckled to herself.

Zara swung at the zombie henchman, who turned with supernatural speed and caught the head of the sledgehammer in his meaty hands. Panic etched her face as she tried to pull the hammer away. The zombie held on to it. Zara tried to yank it back, but her feet slid along the ground as he pulled the weapon toward himself.

I stood and punched the galoot in the head. He didn't notice. I pulled back my fist in pain. It felt like punching an anvil. I looked back at Wally and Garry, who gave me "we're fooked, aren't we?" looks.

For no apparent reason, Zombie Goliath's head twisted to the left as if he'd been socked on the jaw, then jerked to the right. A look of confusion washed over the half of his face still there. He spun, doubled over, and flew into Ilsa.

"Lucius!" Wally shouted. "You came back!" The wizard jumped for joy.

I still didn't see Wally's imaginary friend, but I finally believed in him.

"Auf Wiedersehen," the Nazi doctor said, before she made a gesture with her right hand and vanished along with her henchmen and Oswald.

Wally ran over to an empty spot in the middle of the corridor. "Lucius! You saved us!"

I fell back against the wall, a heat rising up my body. I couldn't move. I kept thinking, "They got Oswald. They fookin got Oswald."

"We'll get him back." Zara put her hand on my shoulder.

"We still need to find the souls," Garry said.

I punched him so hard his wig flew off.

13

WHERE IS MY SOUL?

WHEN WE RETURNED to the surface, hunger and despair tore at my insides. I had never felt anything so black—and I've been tortured by a psychotic Nazi scientist. All seemed lost and pointless. I had no will to continue. I didn't give a gremlin's arse about the souls, no matter what Garry said about them. I hated that skeleton more than I have ever hated anyone before. Well, maybe not as bad as that Nazi bitch and her pet zombie, but pretty close.

Zara kept saying that we'll get Oswald back, we just needed to find the souls first. We had come so far already. "You understand, right?"

I felt like a gutted and filleted merman. It had been months since Oswald wasn't beside me. Old habits die hard. I pulled off my satchel and threw it away.

The world spun. I sat on a boulder away from the others, trying to communicate with Oswald, but received only a dreadful silence. A memory of our first meeting flashed in my mind. The bastard had just oozed from a hole in my skull. A puddle of white liquid pooled at my feet, then morphed into a little man. For months, I had been suffering from the worst migraines in my undead life. The pain had gotten so bad I took a chisel to my pate and opened a hole. That's when Oswald decided to reveal himself. He leaked out of my head like pus out of a pimple.

When he first spoke, I nearly jumped out of my skin. He told me he had been living in my head for six months because he found it warm and cozy in there. He prattled on like he knew me my entire life.

I wanted nothing to do with the creep, but he wouldn't leave me alone. He followed me everywhere, even on cases, which had been scarce back in those days. Eventually, I let him tag along with me, mostly because he seemed so pathetic. Besides, I needed an assistant and he worked for free. He had no name. So I named him Oswald. He had no eyes either. So I scratched two X's in his head and called him a homunculus, a little man. Soon, I'd call him a thorn in my fookin side.

Wally dug another hole in the ground, bent over it, and whispered, doing his old snake bit.

"Why the hell would you trust a snake, Wally?" Zara grabbed the wizard by the shoulder.

He brushed her off. "Trust me. She won't say a thing."

Zara stepped back. "You better be right."

I had the yellow powder half out of my pocket when the snake came slithering toward Wally.

"Sorry, Neba," he said. "We need to find something else."

The snake hissed.

"I know you just helped us, but we're looking for souls that are most likely buried here. They'd be in clay jars."

The snake hissed.

"She wants something," Wally said.

"Like what?" Zara asked. "Not another tonsil manipulation?"

"She wants something shiny this time."

"How about my watch?" Garry said. "I'm not going to need it."

"Perfect."

Garry dropped the timepiece beside her and she swallowed it. Why? I had no idea.

The snake slithered away. Wally and Garry ran after her.

"I'll wait here," I said, but Zara had other ideas. She grabbed me by the back of the neck and pulled me up.

She pushed me along a narrow path flanked by strange brown roots that waved like seaweed underwater. Skeletal tree branches formed an intricate latticework above our heads, blocking off the sky. No wind blew.

Though I had taken dust only a few hours ago, my hunger rolled around in my gut with tsunami-sized waves. My throat burned and my stomach knotted. The snake looked fat and juicy. She'd probably taste like taffy. I even thought of breaking open Garry's bones to get at the marrow.

The snake stopped beside a rotten tree trunk covered in those strange roots, and hissed at Wally.

"She says it's here." Then to the snake, he said, "Let me thank you."

Wally pursed his lips and lowered himself toward the snake. The serpent rose to receive her thank-you kiss, but instead the wizard snatched up the creature and bashed her against the tree trunk.

"Fookin Nazi traitor," he said, as blood spilled onto his

hand. He dropped the dead snake on the ground. "You can have your watch back, Garry."

"I'd rather have my soul." The skeleton dropped to his knees before the tree trunk and dug with his hands. I watched with no interest. I hoped he didn't find the souls. They only led to trouble.

Thoughts of what the Nazis had planned for Oswald entered my head and I had to drive them out.

Garry stopped digging. "I think I found something!" His glee made me want to vomit. "This has to be it." He dug more furiously and soon he lifted up a filthy wooden box about the size of a chessboard. "The fookin souls!" he yelled maniacally. "My fookin soul!"

He laid the box on the ground and carefully lifted the lid. It contained dozens of small clay jars like eggs in a carton. Garry lifted one out and turned it over. He put it back and picked up another. Each had a series of numbers etched on their bottoms, as they did in the journal illustrations.

Garry's eyes went wide. "This is mine! One-one-two-three!"

"Yippee, arsehole!" I said.

"Jack, aren't you excited?" Wally asked. "You're getting your soul back."

"Yippee!" I repeated.

"And here's Jack's," Garry said. He held up a clay jar that looked like all the others. Except this one had 1134 written on it.

"Are you going to kill yourself now, Garry?" I asked, hoping he'd answer in the affirmative.

"Jack, what's the matter? After all these years, we found our souls. You don't have to be a zombie anymore." He put my soul back in the box.

"Maybe I like being a zombie."

"That's your choice, buddy. I don't like being a skeleton."

"Then open your jar."

"I will."

"Good."

His nervousness showed. After all this time, he was unsure. He had been a zombie/skeleton longer than a human. And he had never been much of a human.

He held up his soul vessel and studied it.

"A word of warning," Wally said. "There won't be any turning back once you reunite with your soul."

"I know what I want," he said.

"You don't even know what's going to happen," I said. "It might not be pretty."

"You're not talking me out of this because you're afraid."

Garry took a breath, tilted his head back, and cracked open the jar over his gaping mouth. An ethereal orb of purple light poured out. Garry sucked it in like the ultimate bong hit.

Purple light poured out of every orifice in his skull, and then slid down his body, the light burning through his zoot suit.

Soon a purple glow bathed him and a beatific expression appeared on his face. In a flash, Garry turned human. Flesh and all. A magnificent thick mop of curly blond hair covered his head.

"I'm free," he said, smiling dumbly. "Finally free."

"Your hair looks fantastic," Zara said.

"I know." He stroked it. His blue eyes sparkled. I thought he was about to orgasm. Then his flesh turned transparent and he gently hovered over the ground. I knew that look. My secretary, Lilith, is a ghost, too.

"I guess this is goodbye, buddy," Garry said, "I'm off to the great beyond. I hear it's nice. Good luck finding Oswald." He waved and faded away. Only his elf-hair wig remained, flopped on the ground like a dead beaver.

"Good riddance," I muttered.

"Jack!" Zara slapped me in the back of the head.

"If it wasn't for him, Oswald wouldn't be a Nazi toy now."

"Not his fault, Jack."

"He wanted to find the souls."

"And you found them. What are you going to do with yours?"

I thought about it. I could join Garry in the afterlife. Give up the life of a two-bit detective in this hellscape. It was never much.

Zara handed me my soul jar. It felt a bit lighter than I expected. But souls don't weigh much, do they?

Maybe I could release the damn thing. Send it on its way. What did I need it for?

I examined the vessel. And that's when I noticed a hairline crack around its circumference. I grabbed the top of the jar with one hand and the bottom with the other. A slight twist and the two ends came apart.

Empty.

14

SOULS. WHAT ARE THEY GOOD FOR?

HOW DID I get here?

Nazis stole my soul during WWII. It was the low point of the war. For me, anyway. They had a bit of trouble extracting it. The bastards had to kill me in the secret bunker known as Room 731, over and over, until I finally gave up the ghost. Once Dr. Josef Ratzinger, Nazi psycho extraordinaire, had possession of my lifeforce, I became his obedient zombie slave. Sort of like that Bela Lugosi flick White Zombie. But poor old Bela had nothing on the Nazis. What would a Nazi do with a zombie, you ask? If you have to ask, you don't know anything about Nazis. The scum were losing the war, so they created an army of undead and unleashed us on the enemy. Though the war was in its final stages, we had time enough to do some nasty things. Our first stop: a small village in the French countryside. The place had no strategic value. No enemy soldiers. It should have been left alone. But the village had been marked to serve as a training ground for Ratzinger's pet project, and we did exceedingly well. I've returned to that village many times in my nightmares. But that place was just the beginning of the nightmare. Our band of undead brothers burned through France and Poland and even made it to Germany as the Russians closed in. We pushed the Russkies back. With the Germans gathering other supernaturals to their cause, it looked like they could turn the tide of the war. But the Allies zapped us to Pandemonium.

Once free of Ratzinger and trapped in this infernal dimension, I didn't miss my soul. Not really. A soul is a burden. It weighs you down. A soul holds on to all your hurt and misery. I did all right without it, regardless of what Oswald says. Souls are for losers.

The homunculus always made a big deal about souls. He seemed to think they mattered. I didn't give it much thought until Ratzinger came back into my life. I only agreed to look for mine because I didn't want Ratzinger and his band of psychos to get their hands on it. I didn't have any intentions of getting re-enlisted in his stupid outfit.

But I have to admit all of Garry's talk about souls had gotten my hopes up. I thought getting back my lifeforce would be the answer, that it would change everything. For the positive.

I should have known better.

15

Tripping the Light Fantastic

WHAT A KICK in the soft parts. My dark despair turned darker. My despair turned despairer. I was one fookin sad zombie.

I had lost Oswald and my soul, for the second time.

What did I have left?

Where could my soul have gone? Was it destroyed? Was it wandering around Pandemonium like a lost puppy? Had Ratzinger gotten his hands on it? Did it not want to be found?

And had I found it, what would I do with it?

Would I reunite with my lifeforce and shuffle off to the great beyond like that dimwit Garry? Do I want to leave Pandemonium? To be honest, I feel more at home here than I ever did in the Other World. At least in the Five Cities, I know where I stand: at the very bottom of society.

"Jack, it doesn't mean anything." Zara patted me on the back. "I'm sure your soul is somewhere out there."

I didn't need my soul. I've solved hundreds of cases without it. I saved the world. What did I need a soul for?

I needed only one thing. Dust.

I could always count on the sparkly powder. It always picked me up. Made me feel alive, even on my darkest days. Then I remembered Lucifer's yellow powder in my pocket. Third Circle. The most powerful (and expensive) dust in Pandemonium.

As I removed the baggie, I felt another pang of hunger. My body burned with an unquenchable fire.

"Come on, Jack. We don't have time for this," Zara said. "We have to stop those Nazi bastards. Give me that shit. Dust is for losers."

"In a second."

Zara tried to snatch the dust from me, but I pulled it back.

"Don't fall apart on us," she said. "I can't believe I'm saying this, but we need you."

Zara moved toward me. I ran deeper into the woods, and she chased after me.

"Jack, goddammit, don't take that dust!" Zara screamed. "I'm serious."

I shambled like the dickens, hopping over grabbing vines and tree stumps. The shadows deepened in this part of the wood and the wind made funny sounds.

When I figured I had enough distance between us, I poured out the dust on my fist and took three quick bumps. I leaned against the corpse of a tree. Zara caught up with me. She wore an expression of infinite disappointment. I stared at her for what seemed another infinity. Her face changed, stretching apart like taffy. Her body undulated like waves of heat.

She repeated, "Oh, Jack, oh. Oh, Jack, oh. Oh, Jack, oh."

If I had a heart, it pumped like a mighty steam engine. My body prickled as if covered with fire ants. Who the fook needs a soul when you have fairy dust? I was alive!

The Dire Wood melted away, and I found myself standing in a bright place. Clear blue sky. Yellow sun. Fat white clouds. Dozen of shark women stood before me, dancing the Charleston. They hopped and shimmied on their fins and waved their human arms.

Dance with us, Jack.

I had never had dust like this. This stuff was the real deal.

I'm not a good dancer.

We'll teach you.

Do you know where my soul is?

The shark women flipped up their seaweed skirts. Like what you see?

I ran. No shambling. I ran with power and grace, on human legs.

I moved through a city. Not Pandemonium. Tall buildings crowded the streets. New York City. I stood in the middle of Broadway. Ticker tape covered the ground, as if a great parade or party had rolled through only minutes before. A block ahead, I spotted a woman in a yellow sundress, her long blonde hair waving in the wind as she swiftly turned the corner.

I thought I recognized the woman and ran toward her, shouting her name, though I couldn't understand it in my mind. As I ran, the sidewalk grew longer and I couldn't gain any ground. Wait! Wait! Wait! I shouted. Have you seen my soul? But I knew she couldn't hear me.

I stopped. My surroundings shifted to a dark place, an underground place of stone and fire.

I looked up at Lucifer descending from the shadows. He must have been a hundred feet tall and no longer wore golf clothes. He was naked, his body bright red and hairless. His cloven hooves stamped the ground.

That was some good shit I gave you, huh?

I think I'm in heaven.

The devil laughed and laughed like I just told him the greatest joke.

Is it true you're God, Jesus, and the Holy Spirit?

I think you have me mixed up with someone else.

I don't know what I'm doing anymore.

You're just having a bad trip, Jack. Just keep walking.

I didn't realize it, but I was moving. I looked down at a rainbow beneath my feet. Above me, the red and starless Pandemonium sky.

A leprechaun came skipping toward me. He sang a jaunty tune.

Once there was man named McSweeney...

My old dealer Fine Flanagan walked beside me.

Didn't I eat you once?

You sure did. How did I taste?

I'm not going to lie. You were delicious.

That's all that matters then. Life is too short to sweat over eating a dear old friend. I guess it's my fault for tasting so yummy.

Did I eat your soul, too?

Leprechauns don't keep their souls in their bodies, dummy. It's too dangerous.

I have to go now. I have to walk.

Don't wear out your feet. The lep skipped past me.

I crested the rainbow and descended the far side. A rumbling stirred behind me. When I turned, a giant

Oswald-shaped boulder, rolled toward me. I sprinted with everything I had. My thighs ached and strained. In an instant, I stood motionless. I lifted my legs, but glue covered them. Though I tried harder to move, I couldn't get unstuck. I lifted my legs higher and higher, but the glue rode up to my thighs. The Oswald boulder steamrolled over me, and stopped a few feet away. I stood.

Really, Jack? I'm gone a few minutes and you're already getting high?

Even in my fever dreams, you nag me?

You need nagging. I could do much worse.

You've been gone longer than a few minutes.

I've been by your side all this time, haven't I?

But that wasn't really you. You were sleeping.

The giant Oswald frowned a giant frown.

My soul is gone.

Then find it.

I have no idea where to start. It can be anywhere.

You know better, Jack. Think. You've known for a long time, but you didn't want to admit it. You can be a stubborn fool.

No. No. No.

I had returned to Room 731. Naked. Lying on a steel table. Inside a clear body bag. I looked down at myself.

Ratzinger stood beside a machine with many pumps and moving parts that made sucking noises. He was saying, "We did it! We finally did it!"

Pain washed over me. Excruciating pain. Like I had been skinned alive and dropped in a vat of acid. Then nothing. Numbness. Emptiness. A small ball of light left my still body, sucked up into a hose connected to the machine, and floated away. The machine whirred and whistled and then I floated back into my body, but still felt nothing. My view shifted to looking out from my real eyes, through the plastic body bag.

Ratzinger hovered over me, his grotesque smile inches from my nose. "Welcome back. I am happy to see you are still with us, mein cow-boy."

I closed my eyes, and when I opened them, I stood in water up to my waist.

The shark women circled me, their gray fins cutting the water like sickles. One popped her head over the surface. Georgina, the shark woman who saved me from the Broken Sea, said, You should listen to the homunculus, sweetie. He's a lot smarter than you. Cuter too. She smiled a horrible smile, showing off her dagger teeth.

I waded until I came to the shore. I walked across the beach. The instant my foot hit sand, the world changed, leaving me ascending a staircase in the sky. I looked down at Manhattan. Not ShadowShade, but honest-to-goodness New York City. Exactly as I had left it, no demon cabbies or vampire bankers. No werewolf police officers. Only humans. I thought of the woman I couldn't catch. I tried to remember her name.

You want to go back? Oswald's voice boomed from the heavens.

Of course. But not like this.

If you want to go back, you have to go inside.

Inside where?

Find me.

Where are you?

The Obsidian Tower.

When this is all over, we're going to have a long talk.

Jack, it isn't going to be easy. The interior of the tower is in the fourth dimension.

So what? That's only one more dimension than usual.

Hurry or there'll be no more talking for anyone.

This changes nothing. I still may throw you out of the agency.

Remember, Jack, you don't have to be a zombie if you don't want to be.

An interdimensional baby, his curly hair waving in the breeze, floated by and gave me the finger. Unicorns goose-stepped beside the staircase. Ukobach, the fire demon, flew by jabbing his poker at me. I know Beelzebub, he shouted, and drifted away.

Oswald's voice: Hurry, Jack. They want me to suck up everyone's soul in Pandemonium.

I still hate you, Oswald.

I know.

When I reached the top of the staircase, a red kraken roared up from the depths, its tentacles flailing. It opened its mouth, and kept opening its mouth until it filled the entire sky. I stepped inside and slid down the kraken's smooth-as-glass tongue. I screwed my eyes closed, raised my arms over my head, and yelled, Whee!

When I opened my eyes, Zara's face stood inches from mine. "Where am I?"

"Right where you've been for the last half hour."

"We have to go to the Obsidian Tower. That's where they're holding Oswald."

"How do you know that?"

I stood, straightening my hat. "Fairy dust has never let me down before."

"I have one word for you: rehab."

"And put your damn clothes back on," Wally said to me.

I looked down and, to my horror, I wore my zombie birthday suit.

"What happened?" I asked.

"You just started ripping off your clothes and screaming for Oswald," said Zara. "It was a heck of a sight."

"This has been fun," Wally said, "but Lucius and I have had our fill of adventure."

"I admit there have been some bumps in the road," I said.

"I wish you two the best of luck, but prison isn't so bad. Three squares a day, and all the time to read. I'm too old for Nazis and fairy dust freakouts. Besides, you only needed me to translate your book, and I did that."

"Thanks for the help, especially you, Lucius. You saved our necks back there."

"You're welcome," said a deep, baritone voice that nearly gave me a heart attack.

Wally held out his hand, and an invisible hand took his. They sauntered away.

"And then there were two," I said. "That is, if you're still with me?"

"I couldn't abandon you now," Zara said. "You're like the saddest guy in the history of Pandemonium at the moment. Besides, I haven't gotten to kill the Duke yet."

I dressed and we headed northeast to the Obsidian Tower and certain misery.

16
WELCOME TO NAZI TOWN

DARKNESS SPREAD AS we trekked out of the Dire Wood. The dead trees, wooden corpses frozen in crime scene poses, crowded the narrow path. Black vines, like hairy snakes, twined over the trees and ground. The wood seemed to press in on us. Zara remained on high alert, crouching with her hammer in hand, scanning the area for predators. I lit a hellfire stick and listened to cryptid paws scratching over dry leaves. When the creatures howled, a cold fire licked up my back.

"Are you sure we're going the right way?" I asked.
"I'm making an educated guess," Zara said.
"This is your hometown, isn't it?"
"I haven't been here in many years."
"But you know the place?"
"I was born in New Salem, just south of here. We would sneak into the Dire Wood for short periods, but we never went very far. It's not safe."

We walked on, led only by shadows.

Something large bayed, a deep, guttural call. It was close.

"What are those things?" I asked.

"Wendigos. If you stay on the path, they probably won't attack. They're cowards."

"Then we should get along fine."

I thought I saw eyes glow behind a tree stump. I shambled a bit faster.

The path widened where the edge of the wood met a plain of deep green grass. I had never seen such a lush and idyllic scene in Pandemonium before. The sky burned a bright pinkish-red. It shimmered above our heads like hellfire.

I couldn't enjoy the view. Something pounded inside my head. It must have been the comedown from Lucifer's dust. Nasty, powerful stuff.

"Hard to believe the Nazis live here," Zara said. "This might be the most beautiful spot in Pandemonium."

"It's okay," I said. "But I'd rather be in a formaldehyde bar right now."

The Obsidian Tower rose like a giant shard of black glass from the meadow straight ahead. To the right sat Abracadabra Hill, a smooth brown hump in the distance.

We crossed the plain in silence.

Right about now would usually be the time I'd be thinking of a plan, but my head felt ready to split in half. I tried to communicate with Oswald telepathically, but he didn't answer. Or couldn't. Was that really Oswald who spoke to me in my dust dream? Or had that come from my imagination? *If you want to go back, you have to go inside.* What the heck did that mean? What did any of it mean? *I've known for a long time?* What did I know? And the kicker: Remember, Jack, you don't have to be a zombie if you don't want to be. When you don't have a soul, can't die, and crave flesh, what else does that add up to? I can do the fookin math. It wasn't a matter of not wanting to be a zombie. It was a matter of undeniable facts. Ratzinger stole my soul, turned me into a monster. I've been making the best of it ever since. I didn't need a homunculus to shame me for what I had no power over. But, Jack, you've controlled your flesh craving—more or less—and have become Pandemonium's leading detective, I imagined Oswald saying. Maybe not the last part. I couldn't think any more about this. I had Nazis to deal with.

The plain ended at a plateau overlooking Nazi Town. We got down on our bellies and studied the layout.

The tower stood in the northwest corner of the camp. It must have been a thousand feet high. Three squat buildings clustered together a short distance from the tower, resembling barracks or hangars. Smaller buildings and what looked like a town square sat off to the east. Three main roads cut through the camp, and a massive magic circle drawn in what looked like piles of sand surrounded the entire installation.

"How are we going to get past the circle?" I asked.

"It shouldn't be a problem," Zara said. "It probably only keeps out demons, thus allowing the humans to freely come and go."

"I'm not human."

"Don't be so hard on yourself."

"Neither are you. Not fully."

"I'm human enough and so are you."

"We don't look like Nazis, so that will be a problem. We need to get our hands on uniforms."

"Which means we're gonna have to get our hands dirty."

"There." I pointed at an area near the edge of town where several cars and trucks sat behind a chain-link fence along the southern edge of the camp.

We stumbled down a steep path on the other side of the plateau and stayed low to avoid detection. Several times, I nearly took a tumble on the rocky ground. As we got closer, I got a better look at the vehicles, including several German army trucks, circa WWII. Tanks, too. Lots of cars that looked like vintage BMWs and Mercedes. These Nazi bastards were recreating the Third Reich. Or would it technically be the Fourth Reich? What the hell was a Reich anyway? I'm sure something terrible.

When we came to the edge of the magic circle, I asked, "What do you think it's made of?"

"Looks like cremains."

I looked closer. Chunks of bone and teeth dotted the ashes. "Same old Nazis."

"Neo my arse."

Zara knelt on top of the ash, spoke a few magic words, and touched the fence. The links melted like they'd been covered in acid.

The voices of two men broke the silence.

Before I crossed the circle, I prayed to the Great Unicorn not to be obliterated. Zara slipped inside the camp and encouraged me to follow. I closed my eyes, hopped over the circle, and tumbled through the fence.

"See?" Zara whispered when I reached the other side. "You're more human than you think."

We ducked behind a camouflaged truck. One of the men spoke in German, badly. His pal kept correcting him in English. "It's not Der Katze ist weis. It's Die Katze ist schwarz. Die."

"What's der difference?" the first one asked. "You know what I'm trying to say."

I peered over the hood. Two Nazis in crisp suits smoked hellfire sticks against a snazzy black sedan. I crept back to Zara and whispered, "I'll distract them and you come around the other side."

She nodded.

I pulled my hat down over my eyes, tugged a Lucky Dragon from my pocket, popped it in my mouth, and lit it.

The Nazis prattled on. The one on my left was a big, meaty guy with fists like clubs. The other was short and thin with a crooked jaw, like he took a wrench to the face a few too many times. Crooked Jaw wore mirrored sunglasses and grinned at me.

I didn't like him. "Mir geht's nicht gut?" I asked as I swung around the sedan, the only German phrase I could remember on such short notice.

The shorter one asked, "Who the fook are you?"

"I'm looking to become a Nazi. I mean a neo-Nazi. Gotta keep up with the times, right? Where do I sign up? Who do I have to sieg heil to get a sweet uniform like you fellas?"

"Did someone set you on fire?" the big one asked.

I glanced out the corner of my eye at Zara stalking behind them. "There's a funny story behind that actually. If we had more time, I'd tell you."

"Your cheek is missing," Short Stuff said, a second before Zara's hammer bashed in his temple, went straight through his skull, and smashed the big Nazi's head, too. Two birds... Blood sprayed from their necks like a pair of busted fire hydrants. It didn't ruin my suit. So much blood spatter covered me that it had become part of my suit.

"Couldn't you have done that a little neater?" I asked. "You know how the Nazis are about keeping their uniforms neat."

"Get their clothes off before someone sees us."

"I thought you weren't that kind of girl, Zara."

"Funny."

I kneeled beside the big Nazi. "Turn around."

"It's okay. I've seen it all."

"Fine with me." I bent over the Nazi and dragged my tongue over his jacket, lapping up his blood and chunks of his brain.

Zara threw a hand over her mouth. "Fookin gross! Are you really doing that?"

I wiped my lips with my sleeve. "How else am I supposed to clean up your mess?"

"I'll turn around."

Zara made an about-face and pulled off her armor. I dove back in. The blood had cooled enough to ruin the flavor, but the brains retained enough warmth to spark my taste buds. I salivated as I gulped down the succulent gray matter. It had been years since I chowed down on brain, so my opinion may have been skewed.

Once I had licked those Nazis cleaner than a whistle, save a few stains, I slid the big guy's uniform jacket over my clothes, but not before shoving my fedora into my magic inside pocket and taking out The Book of Three Towers. I put the grimoire in the uniform's breast pocket.

I handed the other uniform to Zara.

"I think I'd rather have worn clothes covered in blood

and brain than zombie drivel." She cringed as she slipped her arms into the brown shirt.

I took the small guy's glasses and slid his cap as far down on my face as possible, hoping I could hide my ugly mug.

We left the carpool.

A commotion erupted in the direction of the town square. People streamed toward the eastern end of the camp in great excitement, hopefully, too excited to notice us. We walked along a gravel road, as far away from the crowds as possible. Gray one-story buildings flanked the road. Nazi flags and banners flew every few feet. For neo-Nazis, they sure didn't change much. The flags were still red and black and white and covered in their beloved swastikas. I didn't know what Nazis loved more: their uniforms or their flags.

A truck barreled down the road kicking up gravel behind us. We jumped out of its way. I thought they had gotten wise to us, but the truck kept flying right on by. A bunch of Nazis stood in the bed waving and shouting like children on the way to the circus.

We followed the truck to the edge of the square.

Dozens of people gathered around a huge bonfire that roared behind a bronze statue of what can best be described as a winged werewolf Hitler. I had to admit it was an improvement. Das führer always reminded me of an angry tax attorney. But this version had muscles and, well, wings. The little postage stamp mustache kinda ruined it.

Black and red banners hung over the buildings circling the square. Torches burned. At the head of the crowd was a platform upon which stood a little man behind a podium. Thankfully, he didn't have a werewolf head or wings, but he did have that creepy mustache, as well as a creepy little mouth that resembled the pucker of a kissing fish. Unlike the Nazis in the crowd, he didn't wear a uniform but a black suit with a swastika armband around his right bicep. It looked like a rally. Great, a Nazi rally.

A hand clamped down on my shoulder. I spun around, my fist cocked. A fat, balding Nazi smiled at me. He looked like he had a sack of potatoes under his brown shirt. He glanced at Zara and grinned wider, his double chin tripling.

"You're missing the festivities," he said, his terrible combover flapping in the wind. "I was late myself. Come on, before there's nowhere to stand."

He didn't wait for an answer. The creep pulled us along and we pressed into the rally. The obese Nazi stood beside me, beaming up at the guy at the podium.

"I've been waiting all week for this," said the fat Nazi while holding up a book. He probably wanted the Nazi's autograph.

A public address system crackled to life, and the man on the podium spoke, his voice booming like a gong.

"The era of monsters is now at an end. The breakthrough of human innovation has again cleared the way on our righteous path. The future human will not be a servant or summoner of demons, but a virtuous man. As a supernatural, to already have the courage to face the unknown, to overcome the limits of mortals, and to triumph over all—this is the task of our cast." He paused and the Children of Thule cheered. "And thus you do well in this midnight hour to commit to the flames the evil spirit of this world and all others to come. This is a mighty and symbolic deed—a deed which shall trumpet to the old world that the infernal and corrupt foundation of Pandemonium is sinking to the ground, but from this wreckage, the phoenix of a new spirit will triumphantly rise. A new age, not of gods and monsters, but of gods and men.

"No to decadence and moral corruption!" He shouted. "Yes to decency and morality in family and state!"

He raised both his arms high and the bonfire flames shot twenty feet above the gathering of Nazis.

From behind the podium, he raised two books. "I consign to the fire the infernal writings of a corruption and decay." He tossed the books into the bonfire and the flames streaked into the burning sky.

"Join me, comrades, in baptizing the grimoires," he said.

The Nazis flung books from all sides, feeding the hungry conflagration. My face burned from the heat.

I never cared much for reading. I had always been a cinema guy myself. Douglas Fairbanks was a personal hero. But I still didn't like this one bit.

The fat Nazi tossed his book into the bonfire. He turned to me. "Where is your grimoire, brother?"

I patted my body and shrugged.

"If the minister discovers that you have kept your grimoire, he won't be happy," the Nazi said. "They're tools of the infernal. Everyone was obligated to bring a grimoire to the burning."

"I must not have gotten that memo. I was kind of busy doing other Nazi stuff."

"Yeah," Zara said. "Nazi-ing is a full-time job. Sieg heiling, polished jack boots, hating stuff."

"I was hating a load of stuff all day," I said. "I was just spitting mad. We should go get a couple of grimoires and come back."

The Nazi jabbed me in the chest with his forefinger.

Thunk! "Sounds like there's a book in your jacket, friend. Feels a bit magical, too."

"That?" I said. "No. It's my personal diary."

"What do you write in it?"

"Mostly my musings. My hopes and dreams for the Fourth Reich."

"The Fourth Reich?" He looked at me queerly.

"The Fifth Reich? I get my Reichs mixed up sometimes."

"What's wrong with your face?"

"Can you be more specific?"

"You're not a zombie, are you? Zombies can't be officers. Why are you wearing that uniform?" He looked closer, reading my nametag. "Captain Gereheart?" The Nazi paused. "Now that I think of it, zombies can't speak."

"I can even count in German. Eins, zwei, drei…" I nodded at Zara, and we started backing up. "I'm heading to my sleeping quarters to get that grimoire. We'll be right back."

The Nazi said, "No. Wait there," then shouted, "Minister Eich, we have—"

I walloped the bastard with a mighty right. I must have really leaned into the haymaker, because the Nazi flew straight into the bonfire. The meatball flailed his arms like he tried to do the backstroke, and then his combover went up like a Roman candle. He must have used a ton of hairspray to keep that thing in place. The flames quickly engulfed his face, and that's when the screaming started. The Nazis turned in our direction.

Then, as so often happens in a situation like this, someone shouted, "Get him!"

Zara's hands fluttered like electrocuted birds. A blinding flash of light exploded in front of us, and like a couple of

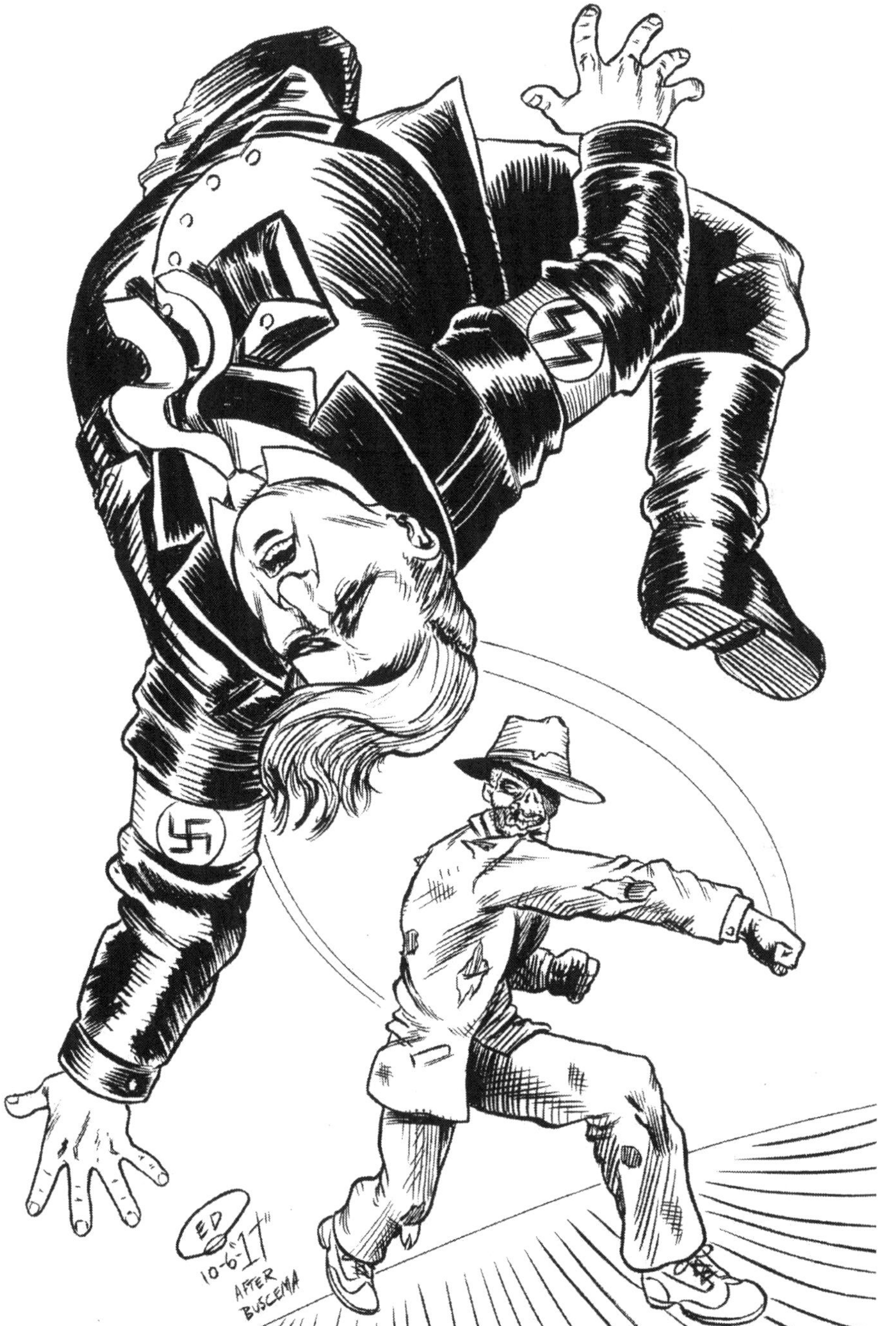
ED
10-6-17
AFTER
BUSCEMA

magicians, we disappeared in a cloud of smoke the pixie/witch had conjured.

We ducked into the first building we came across, which turned out to be a big mistake.

17

CAGED FURY

THOUSANDS MUST HAVE died here. The stench of death and decay filled my nostrils. It mingled with an antiseptic hospital smell, like they had tried to wash away the slaughter, but did a bad job of it.

We stood in a large, brightly lit room. Cracked white tiles covered the floor. Puke green paint peeled from the walls in long strips. An empty gurney and a steel chair stood against the back wall.

I jammed the chair under the doorknob. "That won't hold them for long."

"Come on," Zara said. "Maybe there's a bonfire back here where you can push in all the Nazis."

"Sounds like you're jealous."

"Did you hear that guy scream?"

"Neo-Nazi? More like well-done Nazi." We both laughed. Punching Nazis is fun.

We went through a pair of swinging doors and followed a long hallway past windows that looked into rooms containing surgical tables, medical equipment, and strange machines equipped with thick wires and tubes.

At the sound of approaching footsteps and voices, we turned left into a side corridor.

"So an ogre comes home to find his pixie wife with her suitcases packed in the living room," a woman said.

"I think I heard this one," replied a man.

"'Where the hell do you think you're going?' the ogre says. 'I'm going to ShadowShade. A pixie can earn four hundred gold coins just twittering her wings there, and I figured that I might as well earn money for what I do for you free.'"

Laughter.

Nazi humor.

"In here." Zara pushed open a door and slipped in.

I followed her into a dark and cold room with an earthy smell of hay and shit that reminded me of a stable.

After fumbling around at the wall, I found the light switch and flicked it.

The light revealed a small chamber, a surgical table at its center next to a tall gray machine covered in fat dials and gauges. The smell came from a long, narrow extension leading away from the rear of the chamber, lined with cages.

No lights had come on in the extension, but when I went to pull another lever set in the wall, Zara shouted, "Don't!" I yanked my hand away. "Can't you read?"

A sign next to the lever read, "Emergency cage release," in big, bold letters.

"Oops." On the other wall, I found a second light switch. I flipped it, and the extension glowed with the soft yellow of a dying bulb.

No sound came from the cages, but shadows flickered on the ground.

"What do you think are inside those cages?" I asked.

"I'm sure it's something harmless and perfectly sane." Zara rolled her eyes.

I crossed the room to the extension and peered into the first cage on my right.

I stuck my face close to the bars and instantly regretted it. The stench was stronger here. Sweat mingled with rot. Whatever the Nazis kept in there had been confined for a long time.

"Hello," I said, and gently rapped on the bars. Two yellow eyes blinked open. The creature moved into the light. A goat stared back at me. Its two horns swept back, its ears pointing straight up. The creature crept closer to the bars with a herky-jerky gait, unlike a typical goat. Probably because it wasn't a typical goat. It had a man's torso and legs. The half man, half goat stood on its two legs, gave out a bleat like a child whose throat had been cut, and bashed its horns into the bars.

I jumped back. "I'm not here to hurt you, dunzy."

But the thing kept ramming its head into the bars. The noise caused the occupants of the other cages to awaken. They joined the goat man in banging and rattling their cages. Some howled like sirens.

The knob on the door creaked.

"Go!" Zara rasped.

I power-shambled past a zombie with two heads, a fishman with wings, a half ogre/half orc. All the monstrosities screamed and spit at me.

Even when the Nazis experimented on me back in the war, they hadn't done anything like this. Apparently, they had upgraded their depravity.

Didn't Ilsa Hellstrom say something about hybrids back at the burrow? This must be what she was talking about. I thought of poor Oswald. Lucifer said they wanted him to power a soul sucker. Did they plan to create a homunculus/soul sucker hybrid?

The door at the end of the hall was locked. I kicked it, but it didn't budge. Zara laughed at me.

"I can try, can't I?" I said.

She threw her shoulder at it and the door burst open onto an operating theater. I jumped inside, but I didn't get much of a look at the place, because I came face to rotting face with Zombie Goliath. He tossed me down a flight of stairs that led to a surgery table at the center of the room. My head spun. Nazi zombies swept through the theater, lurching up the tiered rows.

Zara charged in, her hammer swinging. Undead Nazi skulls burst on impact, spraying dark blood onto the walls and ceiling. She spun and slid and hopped around the zombies delivering deathblows from every angle. Yet dozens of reanimated corpses continued to shamble toward the whirling Ms. Moonbeam, numbers their only strength.

Zombie Goliath—seven feet of decayed flesh—lumbered down the stairs. The thick cords in his neck pulsed and looked ready to burst. He must have been steaming mad after that Lucius business back in the burrow.

Back in the Other World, I had been a two-time Golden Gloves champ. My fancy footwork and iron jaw got me a reputation as a real brawler. I could have gone professional if not for the draft. But I never fought a monster. Zombie Goliath might have been stronger than me. And faster. And way over my weight class. But I had a big advantage. Brains. As far as zombies go, I'm Einstein. I wasn't worried.

"No honor among zombies?" I asked after awkwardly getting to my feet.

Zombie Goliath grunted.

I frantically looked for a weapon. "Listen, dunzy, you're dealing with a superior class of zombie. I don't want to send you to the absolute death, so maybe we can work something out."

He grinned with his black jagged teeth as he stepped onto the operating floor.

"It doesn't have to be like this." I pointed at my chest and then at Goliath, to illustrate my point. "We're brothers. You're breaking an age-old code." The code didn't exist, but I hoped he didn't know that.

I grabbed a silver bone mallet and flung it at him. It bounced ineffectually off his barrel chest. I power-shambled around the operating table and headed back up the theater. Zombie Goliath came after me. Zara had already laid out most of the zombie horde, working her way around the room.

I reached the top level when Goliath grabbed me in a bear hug. He squeezed me like an anaconda. I slammed my head back, cracking him square in the face. He released me and I dropped to the floor. I stood, and threw a right, then a left. For good measure, I unloaded an uppercut, connecting with Goliath's jaw. The galoot grinned and walloped me on my iron jaw, launching me through the open door.

I landed on my arse and went skidding between the hybrids' cages.

I reminded myself that my superiority came in the form of my higher intellect. But for the life of me, I couldn't figure how that benefited me at the moment. I rose drunkenly.

The winged fishman hissed at me.

I'd be in a hell of a bind if that thing got out. Then I thought, "What a great idea."

I shambled to the other end of the cages as Zombie Goliath squeezed himself past the doorway at the end of the narrow alcove. He had gotten to the middle of the cages when I reached the emergency release lever and yanked it. All the cages snicked open.

The hybrids bolted from their prisons and tackled Goliath. He managed to toss a few of them across the room, but their numbers overwhelmed him. Goliath continued to throw punches as the abominations smothered him. The sounds of his flesh tearing and his bones breaking reminded me of a buffet I had once attended on the Zombie Islands.

It was a brilliant idea, except for one problem: I'd blocked myself off from getting back into the theater and helping Zara.

The hybrids seemed awfully focused on eating Zombie Goliath, so I took a chance. With a running start, I dashed toward the feeding frenzy. Like a frog, I hopped on the distracted hybrids' heads and backs. They paid me no mind and continued feasting on the buff corpse.

I re-entered the amphitheater…and skidded to a halt in shock.

All the Nazi zombies lay dead—well, truly dead. But Zara had gotten herself into some trouble. Ilsa Hellstrom had appeared and pinned the pixie/witch against the wall beside the door. Thick, slimy tentacles poked out from her uniform. One of them wrapped around Zara's waist and another wrapped around her throat.

Zara spotted me and shouted, "Jack! She's a freak with tentacles!"

Before I realized it, a wormy appendage lashed out and snaked around my body.

"Not a hugger, Jack?" the Nazi bitch asked.

18

Not Another Psycho Nazi Doctor

"**BIG BAD NAZI** scientist in the room. Dun-dun-DUN!" Ilsa Hellstrom bellowed and stood over me, her face silhouetted by a bright surgical light directly behind her.

Me and Zara awoke to find ourselves strapped to a pair of surgical tables in the theater. Leather thongs secured our arms and legs. They left us in our Nazi uniforms. Maybe as punishment.

"You Nazis are like bad pennies," I said.

"We never go out of style," Ilsa said. "Are you comfortable?"

"I've been in worse situations."

"I feel like you should be less comfortable. That feels more Nazi-ish, you know. Maybe I should have put spikes underneath you or something. I'm still new at this."

"Being a psycho?"

"No, silly, a Nazi. I've been a psycho for as long as I can remember. I used to pull the wings off infernal flies and glue them onto worms."

"Your daddy couldn't afford a doll?" Zara said.

"My father called me deranged. His deranged little girl. I had always thought it was a compliment. When I found out he didn't mean it as a compliment, I did worse to him than I did to those flies."

"I'll stick to calling your Dr. Ilsa Hellstrom," I said.

"When you're named Ilsa Hellstrom, you pretty much have to become a Nazi, amiright?"

"Is that what brought you into the fold?"

"Not really. The uniforms mostly."

"I told you," I said to Zara.

"How do I look?" She stood back and did a twirl that ended with a sieg heil.

"You got that fascist look down pretty well," Zara said. "Miss Reichstag 1939."

"Oh, thank you. I wish I had been there in the Other World back then. I heard it was a real humdinger. I'm a stickler for authenticity. Do you guys have a favorite cryptid?"

She moved away from the light and I got a better look at our deranged little Ilsa. She once again had two normal arms and legs, no tentacles I could see.

"A what?" Zara asked.

"Cryptid? Supernatural creature? Bigfoot? Loch Ness Monster, that sort of thing? I'm partial to the kraken," she said. "They're so graceful and strong."

"Is that what you are, a kraken?" I asked.

"A hybrid."

"I thought you Nazis didn't like supernaturals."

"We like supernaturals fine, just as long as we control them. Some supernaturals have amazing abilities. Even this overgrown pixie."

"Watch it, blondie," Zara said. "Seriously."

"She's a pistol, isn't she? You're a hybrid already, though I can't see the pixie in you. Do you have wings?"

"I have a little birdie for you. In case you can't see, I'm giving you the finger."

"It doesn't matter. I can give you wings. Or maybe I can wed you with a troll. You seem like you'd take to it well."

"When I get off this table, I'm going to unwed your head from your neck."

"You're going to be a good Nazi…after you lose a few pounds. I don't think we have a uniform that'll fit a woman of your girth."

Zara bucked like a wild bull. The surgical table lifted off the ground.

"Why don't you let her go?" I asked. "You have me and Oswald."

"Do I look like a nice person?" Ilsa raised an eyebrow. "We have big plans for all of you. Oswald is already in place. You two are just the icing on the cake."

Something boiled in my chest. "If you hurt Oswald—"

"Hurt Oswald? Ha-ha-ha. We've improved him. Just as we're going to improve you two."

"What did you do to Oswald?"

"I wedded him to a soul sucker. There were barely any complications. The Jupiter Stone inside the homunculus is powering the creature, so he can suck up every soul in Pandemonium. Then we're going to have some real fun. What should we wed you with?"

"Why do you care?"

"It takes better if you're willing."

"How about your mother?"

"No, something powerful but more compliant. My mother was a bitch."

"The apple doesn't fall too far from the bitch tree."

"You're weak, Jack. You know it. We all know it. But I can make you stronger. An alpha zombie. How does that sound? You're going to lead the most powerful army of the undead in history. People will look up to you. Now, they just pity you."

"Those things you have in cages don't look powerful," Zara said. "They look insane."

"They were my first attempts. I've gotten much better at it. Then again, you two might go insane, too. It's a chance I'm willing to take. You don't mind giving your bodies to science, do you?"

"Does it hurt?" I asked.

She faux grimaced. "Only constantly."

"Then we'll pass."

"Oh, that's a shame. I was hoping you'd be reasonable."

"Reason isn't our strong suit."

"Now, what would a Nazi do in this situation?" She tapped on her skull. "How would a Nazi get her subjects to see the light? Think, Ilsa, think."

"You could torture us." I said.

"Jack!" Zara shouted.

"I'm not divulging any secrets," I said.

"I really do like you, Jack," Ilsa said. "I have a thing for zombies. It's a shame you're going to lose that moxy. How should I torture you? What's the Naziest thing I could do? I want to get it right."

"Let's see, the last time a Nazi tortured me... I had been drowned, electrocuted, deprived of sleep, impaled by hot pokers..."

"This is good. Should I be writing this down? No, I'll remember. Go ahead."

"I was covered in gasoline and set on fire."

"Oh, that's good. Very Nazi. Was that the worst thing they did?"

"No."

"What was the worst?"

"Water torture."

"That doesn't seem so bad."

"I'm terrified of the water. It freaks me out."

"Oh, perfect. I think we have a water tank somewhere. But I do like the idea of setting you on fire, especially her. I'd like to see those hideous tattoos go up in flames. Why would you do that to your body?"

Zara didn't say anything, probably turning over in her mind how she would kill Ilsa Hellstrom if given another chance.

"Fire is too easy," I said, "too fast, but if you want to go the easier route, we won't think you're any less a Nazi."

She smirked. "If you're going to be a Nazi, be a Nazi, right? No use going only halfway."

"I admire your determination."

"Don't go anywhere. I'll be right back, and while I'm gone, think about what cryptid you want to be. Maybe a chupacabra for the portly pixie?"

When Ilsa left the room, Zara said, "Jack, you really are crazy. Why would you encourage her to torture us?"

"I was buying us some time. I've nearly got my left hand severed."

"Your old 'yank the hand off' trick, huh?"

"It's worked before."

I continued to work my hand at the restraints. My hand was never held on that good. It only needed a bit of coaxing to detach.

"And what do you plan to do once you're free? There's an army of Nazis out there."

"I haven't figured that out yet."

A pop rattled my wrist bone. I twisted my hand and—rip—it came off and fell on the floor. I pulled my stump out of the restraints and held it up. "I'm free! Now I just have to wait until my hand crawls up here."

A clattering came from under the table, but my hand went silent. "It must be stuck."

"Great. How are you going to undo the other restraints with just a stump?"

I thought about that for a moment and a brilliant idea hit me. "I don't need to. I have The Book of Three Towers."

Fortunately, the chips in my wrist bone gave me enough purchase to fiddle with the button on my front pocket. Once I popped it open, sliding out the book was child's play. I pushed the book onto my chest. Now I had to open it.

"I don't think this is a good plan." Zara bucked and thrashed, trying to break free from her restraints, but it did no good. To work her magic, Zara needed to use her hands.

When I tried to open the book, I accidentally flipped it over and it slid down my chest. I feared that it, too, would fall on the ground. I didn't think it would be a good thing if the Nazis got their hands on the book, especially since it held secrets about the towers. Good thing Ilsa didn't search us. She must have been too anxious to torture us. I stopped the book from sliding and pulled it back up to my chin. Something stuck to the back cover. The card Lucifer gave me in his office. I hadn't read it back there.

"For a Really Good Time, Call Lucifer. Anytime. Just tap three times on the card and say 'O, Lucifer, My Lucifer.'"

What's that saying? The enemy of my enemy is my friend. We were no match for an army of Nazis. We needed our own army. And I did believe Lucifer when he said he was only interested in maintaining the status quo in Pandemonium. But then again, he was the Devil—lowercase or uppercase, it didn't matter. Nazis or demons. Demons or Nazis. A heck of a choice.

"What are you doing?" Zara asked. "She's going to be back any minute to torture us and then turn us into goat people or something."

"I'm weighing the lesser of two evils."

"What?"

"I have Lucifer's card. I can summon him."

"You're not really thinking of doing that?"

"Lucifer wants to get rid of the Nazis just like we do. If I summon him, he should be able to get past the magic circle. Right?"

"Possibly. Magic circles can keep things out or you can summon things into them. But whether or not it works isn't the problem. Being in league with the Devil is usually a bad idea. In what kind of crazy world is Lucifer the good guy?"

"We're about to find out." I shoved The Book of Three Towers back in my pocket, and tapped on the card three times. "O, Lucifer, My Lucifer."

THE DEVIL WEARS NADA

HISTORICALLY, DEALS WITH the Devil have been one-sided affairs. The Infernal One isn't known for his fairness or honesty, but since you can count on his duplicity, that makes him highly predictable. The Devil might be a genius, and I might be an idiot, but—actually I don't know where I was going with that. Maybe this was a bad idea. I didn't have any tricks up my sleeve. I was desperate, and it was too late to second-guess myself.

The Man appeared like a rabbit out of a magician's hat. He reeked of sulfur and sex and wore a red satin robe inappropriately open down to his crotch. He also dripped with sticky, wet blood.

"This better be good," Lucifer said. "I was in the middle of a blood orgy and the virgins just showed up."

"The Nazis are about to be experiment on us," I said.

"So? You ever hear the saying 'What doesn't kill you makes you stronger'?"

"I'm proof that's complete bullshit."

"How about you?" Lucifer asked Zara.

"This wasn't my plan," she said.

"Free us before that psycho Nazi doctor gets back," I said.

"Sorry, buddy boy. Summoning doesn't work like that. Quid pro quo is the name of the game. The Devil likes to make bargains." He rubbed his hands together. "Let's make a deal."

"Do you mind if I ask a question first?"

"Shoot."

"Can you explain the infernal trinity? We were having a debate with Syd, who insists you, Beelzebub, and Satan are the same person."

"It's kind of complicated—"

"Yeah, exactly."

"Look at it this way. The Devil is one, undivided 'thing' but three 'beings.' Or they are not each other. They are all the Devil."

"That's what Syd said. I still don't get it."

"How about this? The Devil works in mysterious ways."

"Religion is such bullshit."

"Can we make this damn deal already?" Zara shouted. "Or just let the Nazis experiment on us. I'm getting fed up with the stupidity."

"Name your deal and I'll name my price," Lucifer said.

"You can take the Jupiter Stone from Oswald," I said. "If you promise not to hurt him."

"All you have to do is free us and kill all these Nazi bastards," Zara said.

"That goes without saying," Lucifer said. "But you don't have Oswald. How can you make any bargain?"

"I know where he is. I can get him. Leave that to me."

"I want more than that."

"You can have Zara's soul."

"Jack, you piece of shit!" Zara said.

"After you die, I meant. That's how it usually works, right?"

"No thanks. She's more trouble than she's worth," Lucifer said. "I want The Book of Three Towers. It is mine after all, and you don't really know how to use it. Deal?"

He was right on both counts. I came into possession of the book from a dust junkie who needed cash. He never mentioned it belonged to Lucifer. I still would have bought it, but I would have offered much less for it. "Will you throw in a gram of Third Circle?"

"No problem."

"I guess I'm in league with the Devil then. Do we shake? Do I kiss your arse? What?"

"Usually, there's a contract written in blood. I have my lawyers look it over. There's a whole process. But considering there's a time constraint, I'll waive it. Let's just promise to be fair to each other."

"Cross my heart," I said. What he didn't see was that the fingers on my severed hand were crossed.

He waved at our restraints and they sprang opened.

I hopped off the cold steel table. When I landed on the floor, a few vertebrae popped in my back. I'd pay for that later. I picked up my hand and popped it back on my wrist.

"Can you close your robe?" Zara asked. "I'm seeing way too much Lucifer for my comfort."

"You should count yourself lucky, baby girl," Lucifer said. "Not many women get to see me in all my glory and live to tell about it."

"Don't mess this up," I whispered in Zara's ear.

"I'll count myself lucky then," Zara said.

"Now stand back." Lucifer cracked his knuckles. "It's about to get a bit crowded in here."

20

THAT DARN, MOTHERFOOKIN CAT

CONJURING A DEMON is old hat. It's like Occult 101. An incantation. Fire. Candles. Blood. Mirrors. Graveyard dirt. A goat comes in handy sometimes. Or if you're lucky, you get Lucifer's calling card, like I did. But watching Lucifer himself conjure a demon is something to behold.

The Lord of Hell said, "When he appears, try to act frightened. He thinks he looks all kinds of fearsome, but he's really a pussycat. And really go deep with the 'oh you fookin scared me.' Got it?"

We had no idea what he was talking about, but we nodded.

Lucifer stood in the middle of the surgical area. "You may want to avert your eyes, Zara. This usually gets me excited," Lucifer said, and his robe fell to the ground. The Devil stood naked, the fresh blood covering his skin glistening under the surgical lights. He was much hairier than I expected.

"Let me check my pulse," she said. "Oh, look, I'm still alive."

Lucifer held up his left hand. A hazel wand, a thin and crooked thing, appeared between his thumb and forefinger. He struck the wand at the ground. "By the name of Lucifer—Lord of Darkness, Emperor of the Abyss, Son of the Dawn, and One Crazy Motherfooker... I call you, O mighty Beleth, the terrible—but in a good way—King of Hell." His voice, lower than low and dripping with darkness, reverberated throughout the theater. His body burned the bright red of arterial blood. He pointed his wand at the rows of seats rising up from the theater floor. "Powerful and fearsome"—Lucifer winked at us—"Beleth, who strikes terror in the hearts of the brave with only a glance. Beleth, whose terrible visage is enough to make an angel quiver." Lucifer pointed the wand straight down. "Come to me, Beleth, and do not tarry—even if you're busy with some other bullshit. I have other things to do today."

The room shook as if hit by an earthquake. The air grew stale and oppressive, filled with the music of off-tune brass instruments and out-of-sync drums. It sounded like a funeral march played under water.

First appeared six demons with huge heads and little bodies, their bellies bloated and gray. They played pipes and clanged cymbals. One had a little xylophone that he hit with chicken bones.

Lucifer rolled his eyes. "There's a whole thing he does. But bear with me. He's good."

Another six demons identical to the last appeared in the second row. They played drums, each a different rhythm. Several more of the grotesque musicians popped into the theater. A wild cacophony filled the room. I covered my ears, but Lucifer shook his head at me, so I uncovered them.

Finally, as the music reached its crescendo, my ears bleeding blood I didn't know I had, Beleth appeared at the top of the theater, riding a pale horse. He didn't strike fear in my heart. He resembled a giant tomcat. Tawny fur covered his face, and he had pointy ears and little sharp teeth. Maybe if you came across him in a dark alley unexpectedly you'd jump, but he certainly didn't sound like the fearsome demon who made angels quiver.

Beleth wore dark armor as did his horse, whose huge flared nostrils spit black smoke. The horse, I had to admit, sent shivers down my spine.

The hellion walked his infernal steed down the theater stairs as the music reached a crescendo.

The demon king stood before us, his horse stinking like rotting meat.

Me and Zara and held our heads to the ground.

"Look how they tremble in fear," Beleth intoned, when the music came to an end. I didn't tremble. I glanced at Zara. She didn't tremble either. "Is the mighty Beleth too terrifying that you cannot look upon his visage?"

"They're absolutely terrified," Lucifer said. "Right, guys?" We mumbled in the affirmative. "Guys?"

"We're too afraid to speak." I nudged Zara.

"Yes, I am very scared," Zara said.

Beleth laughed a deep, fake laugh. "Cowards. You are right to fear Beleth."

Why do all the psychos refer to themselves in the third-person?

"You still have those eighty-five legions of demons under your command?" asked Lucifer.

"Eighty-two," Beleth said. "I had to dismiss three legions for being in tune. You know how I feel about music."

"You hate it."

"It's a ridiculous thing, isn't it? But it has a certain effect on the creatures."

"Let me give you a quick rundown. What I want you to do is kill everyone in this camp."

"I can do that."

I coughed.

"Except those two over there, of course. But everyone else is fair game."

"Any particular way you want them executed. Slowly, eaten alive, flayed?"

"Just get rid of them."

"Can I play my jams?"

"Play that jazzy number."

"Oh yes, 'Bitch's Brew.' Perfect choice. You heard Lu, boys. And a one, and a seven…"

The big-headed musicians blasted a racket of noise that didn't sound much different from the last discordant song they played. They lined up in two rows and marched up the theater stairs and out the door. Beleth followed on his pale horse bopping his head right and left.

"Don't forget our deal," Lucifer said to us. He glanced down at his crotch and then smiled at Zara. She rolled her eyes, and Lucifer vanished.

"Geez, the Devil's a creep," she said.

We followed Beleth out of the building as the band headed east. Beleth galloped alongside his band, waving what looked like a conductor's baton. Wherever he pointed the thing, a legion of demons popped into existence. These suckers weren't small like the musicians. They were the size of mountain boulders and walked as if angry at the ground.

Soon they came upon some Nazis. It wasn't pretty. Beleth's demons lifted up the Nazis and tore them apart like paper dolls.

Beleth pointed his conductor's baton at the sky and a legion of winged demons appeared. The creatures, thin and aerodynamic, their beaks like broadswords, searched the ground with hungry eyes. They descended on the camp. The discordant music mingled well with the screams erupting throughout the place. And the explosions added a nice, but chaotic rhythm. Klaxons sounded and vehicles came to life. Fires sprang up in every direction.

"I think they have things under control," I said. "Let's head to the tower."

"I almost feel sorry for those Nazis," said Zara.

21

THIS IS YOUR HORRIBLE LIFE

ALL HELL LITERALLY broke out as we headed to the Obsidian Tower. Demons filled the sky and marched through the camp. The Nazis had been caught off guard, most likely because they never suspected Lucifer to get past their magic circle.

Someone fired a bazooka and a ten-foot-tall demon in the form of a wasp went spinning out of the sky. On his way down, he clipped an antenna atop a roof, which came crashing down mere inches from our feet. The demon landed not far from the antenna, his thin insect legs broken. He managed to lift his triangular head, but slumped to the ground, dead.

"Ever play football?" I asked Zara as we dashed around the fallen demon.

"Can't say I have."

"Then just run in a zig-zag pattern and try not to get hit by any falling Nazis or demons."

A Jeep roared around a building, firing a Gatling gun

mounted in the back. Zara pulled up her sleeve, muttered something, plucked a grenade from her left forearm, and tossed it under a nearby truck. The explosion caught the tail end, flipping it over.

"Or you could do that."

"Come on," Zara said.

We stuck as close to the buildings as we could and made our way across the camp.

More demons appeared above us. The Nazis had finally mounted a counterattack, unleashing their monster army. I recognized a few of the creatures from Skull Mountain. After our little battle over the Pandemonium Device, Ratzinger had sent his soul suckers to suck up the souls of the dead. Zombie demons, gargoyles, sphinxes, and even a couple of unicorns took to the skies. Beleth and his legions met the slave troops with a ferocious force, driving straight into their ranks with claws and fangs and hooves. The Pandemonium heavens dripped with black and red blood.

When we reached the northwestern edge of the camp, we found ourselves alone. The Obsidian Tower, black and mirror smooth, stood a hundred yards in front of us.

"There's no one guarding the tower," I said.

"Doesn't that concern you?"

We hung back, scanning the area. The area was deserted, while the battle raged at the other end of the camp. Beleth pushed the Nazis farther east, the explosions and tortured screams fading in the distance.

"I think they have more pressing concerns, don't they?" I asked.

"Ready then?"

"Not really."

We broke for the tower, a thousand feet of volcanic glass rising into the hellfire sky.

Zara was well ahead of me, naturally. I herked and jerked like a newborn gremlin trying to learn the Charleston. It looked like smooth sailing—until that Nazi bitch came bouncing over the dirt in a Mercedes. She gripped the wheel with white fists, grinning like a maniac. I yelled something like "Look out!" It wasn't too effective. The edge of the front bumper clipped Zara and she rolled over the hood and onto the ground.

Before I could catch up to the fallen pixie/witch, Hellstrom had came to a stop and jumped out of her vehicle. She carried a large weapon, a bazooka perhaps. But as I got closer I realized it wasn't a bazooka. Tentacles streamed out from slits in her uniform and undulated like drunken snakes doing the mambo.

Zara climbed to her feet, her sledgehammer already gripped in both hands, the light glinting off its well-used head.

Zara stared down Ilsa.

"I knew the zombie was an idiot," the Nazi said. "But I had higher hopes for you, Zara. You made a deal with Lucifer? Historically, that's a terrible move. You should have sided with us."

"Lucifer isn't such a bad guy," Zara said. "Some even say he's the hero of the Bible."

"Those people are called Satanists."

"And Nazis are better?"

"Sweetheart, we're not creating hell, we're creating heaven."

"Semantics."

"You could have been perfect like me."

"What the hell are you? A Nazi-ken? A Krakenazi?"

An apocalyptic crack of thunder hammered the sky. The ground shook. I looked up at the top of the Obsidian Tower aglow. In the far distance, thousands of tiny lights came streaming toward the camp. A soul sucker squawked, a high piercing call.

The sucking had commenced.

"Save Oswald," Zara shouted. "I'll handle this bitch."

"You sure?" I said.

"Go!"

"She beat you before."

"She surprised me. I wasn't counting on tentacles."

"I don't want this to be a thing between us. Like I abandoned you or something."

"We're good." Zara ripped off her brown Nazi shirt, exposing a sleeveless T-shirt underneath with "Fook You" written across the chest. Magical tattoos of whips, wands, swords, and potions covered her exposed arms. "This time I'm ready."

I headed to the Obsidian Tower as Ilsa's tentacles whipped at Zara, grabbing hold of her hammer. Ilsa pulled the witch/pixie toward doom, but Zara had other plans. She yanked on her hammer, drawing it back with all her strength, the cords in her neck bulging, and lifted the Nazi hybrid off her feet. She landed in the dirt face first, releasing her grip on Zara's hammer.

I power-shambled to the base of the Obsidian Tower, hoping Zara could handle Ilsa.

The base of the tower must have been at least a quarter of a mile around. I circled it twice, but found no entrance. In fact, I didn't see so much as a crack or crease. The entire tower seemed to have been made of a single piece of solid obsidian. I took out my handy-dandy grimoire. What did Wally call it? LST. Location-specific textuality. If it had info about the Lucifer Tower in Syd's Lair, I prayed it said something about entering the Obsidian Tower now that I stood before it.

I opened the magical text, which pulsed in my hand. I thought I had flipped to a random page. But right in front of me, in bold letters:

On Entering the East Tower

Three Towers
Of Bone
Of Smoke
Of Glass
Earth
Heaven
Spirit

Black as the abyss
Look
It looks at you
Trace your origin
To your final decision

A fookin riddle. I hate riddles.

I looked at my reflection in the surface of the tower. It wasn't a great sight, even for a corpse. My Nazi uniform was in tatters, splattered with blood. My face looked deader than usual, pale and tired. The past few hours had taken a toll on me.

My image did a funny thing. It shook its head. I wasn't

shaking my head. I checked. The zombie in the mirror continued shaking its head, as if telling me I shouldn't enter.

I went over the riddle.

Black as the abyss

The surface is black.

Look

I looked.

It looks at you

That guy in the reflection was certainly looking at me.

Trace your origin

Trace? I touched the surface, as Syd touched the tunnel wall to reveal the Angel Gate.

My image nodded.

I got it. I put the book back in my pocket and traced my reflection with my right forefinger, going clockwise. As I did so, an indentation burned into the obsidian, its edges melting into lava. When I finished, a perfect Jack shape had been etched into the tower.

I removed the Nazi jacket, pulled my fedora from my inner pocket and fixed it back on my head. Now I was ready.

I leaned against the Jack shape and the surface gave. I pushed forward and entered the Obsidian Tower.

When I got to the other side, the hole sealed itself behind me.

To your final decision

I didn't know what that would be, but I didn't like the sound of it.

The inside of the tower seemed much bigger than I had imagined from the outside. Like the exterior, the floor and walls were black glass. A staircase spiraled up the back wall, the only thing in the room.

I took a step forward and a spotlight shone down on me. A fanfare of music broke the silence. "Welcome, Jack, to your…hell," a voice boomed. It took me a moment to recognize Ratzinger. That deep, cocky voice.

"Ratzinger," I said, "is that you, you Nazi bastard? Whatever you've done with Oswald—"

"Oswald is in good hands. We are up here waiting for you, Jack."

"This place doesn't have an elevator?"

"Sorry. You will have to walk up the stairs. It will give us more time."

"What makes me think it'll be a shitty time?"

"Because you are a smart corpse. Always were. That is why I like you so much."

I crossed the room and climbed the staircase, the spotlight following me.

"Now let us get back to our regularly scheduled program." Ratzinger's voice crackled over what sounded like a bad P.A. system. When I reached the second level, the stairs disappeared behind me. "There is only way for you, Jack. Up!"

The spotlight cut out. The level was dark and felt infinite in size. Didn't Oswald say the tower existed in the fourth dimension? What did that mean?

"We are going back to the beginning, Jack. Meet some old friends. I know they are dying to see you again. Ha-ha-ha."

Ratzinger had gotten corny since his resurrection.

The darkness dissolved like smoke in a windstorm. Gradually, a dirt road revealed itself. Light spread into the world, revealing bombed-out buildings, rubble, and ashes. The façade of a church somehow remained with nothing behind it, a hollowed-out building. Farther up the road, a Panzer tank burned.

I stood in the middle of the road, the sun shining bright yellow in a blue sky.

I recognized the place, the French village of Oradour-sur-Glane, the site of the worst massacre in dear old World War II. This was Ratzinger's first test of his undead army. It was a smashing success.

Shadows lengthened and stretched in the corners and hidden places.

Something dark crawled into the road, ahead of the church and slunk toward me like a giant worm. I didn't move. The slug lifted its head, dark blood dripping from its mouth. But it wasn't a slug. It was a man. He pulled himself along the road with arms that had been cut off at the elbow. His legs were missing, as was his lower half. Blood and guts poured out of his exposed torso.

The others rose from the rubble and crawled out from under wrecked cars. Some seemed to rise out of the dirt itself. All had missing limbs, missing flesh. They weren't the undead. They were the food of the undead.

Ratzinger had sent us into this idyllic village, which had no strategic value to the Germans. There were no soldiers here, only simple farmers.

Ratzinger set us loose at sunrise, the sky layered in pale pink and red and yellow.

We had never fed on living flesh before. He kept us like starving mongrels, stoking our hunger for this moment. He didn't need to control us that day. Our hunger drove us and we feasted.

The citizens of Oradour-sur-Glane, their bodies torn open and spilling their contents, surrounded me.

"Is this how you're going to torture me!" I shouted at Ratzinger. He didn't answer.

The villagers stared at me with dead, sunken eyes. I had seen those eyes many times in my dreams. Though what I had done here disgusted me, the old hunger blossomed in my rotten guts. My stomach clenched like a fist, my jaw flexed. I found myself staring at the glistening organs, and realized the Frenchmen didn't want revenge. They offered themselves to me. They pressed forward, holding up their intestines and livers and hearts.

Manger, they said. Manger.

That was Ratzinger's game. Get me to act like a zombie.

You don't have to be a zombie, Jack. Oswald was an idiot. You couldn't decide not to be a flesh eater, just as he couldn't decide not to be an annoying runt. His words didn't have special meaning because they came to me in a dust-fueled dream.

No matter what I did, I remained a zombie. I craved flesh. I had no soul. I smelled like a garbage fire. But Ratzinger wanted me to be his zombie. I couldn't let that happen. Dust! I could kill my hunger with dust. I reached into my pocket.

I was tapped out. Not even a granule of Third Circle.

You were never a good zombie, Jack.

Is that you, Oswald?

No answer.

Was is my imagination? Did it matter? I had heard enough of Oswald to know what he would say at all times. He wasn't that original. I thought of another thing the homunculus said after I took the Devil's dust.

You've known for a long time, but you didn't want to admit it.

Did he really say that, too, or had I lost my mind?

A woman approached me. She held up her beating heart in her blood-slicked hand.

I had to admit it looked appetizing.

I looked into the woman's face. Her eyes were black pebbles, her cheeks sunken and gray.

I knocked the heart out of her hand, pushed her aside, and ran through the village as the citizens of Oradour-sur-Glane chased me, throwing their organs and limbs at me. Hunger burned me, but I kept going until I stood once again in the dark.

The spotlight hit me.

A staircase appeared.

I ascended.

When I reached the second level, faint music played from a radio. I followed the noise, wondering what new torture Ratzinger had in store for me.

The music grew louder. Glenn Miller. My insides twisted. But it had nothing to do with hunger. A dim light appeared in the middle of the darkness.

As I got closer, a couch and a low table came into view. An end table and lamp stood beside a Philco radio atop a scarred and battered credenza. One of its missing legs had been replaced with a brick.

I recognized this scene, too. I stood outside the cozy little domestic setup, hiding in the shadows, as the music bopped and jumped.

From the other end of the room, a woman emerged from the darkness. She ran toward me, her arms held out.

"No," I said.

She stopped, a disappointed and confused look on her face.

"What's the matter, Jack?" she asked, concern in her voice.

I lowered my head and noticed my hands. I turned them over, studied them. I couldn't believe it. The bones didn't show. The flesh wasn't desiccated and burned. I ran my fingers over my face. I no longer had a hole in my cheek. My skin felt soft and supple. Blood coursed through my veins.

I wasn't Dead Jack anymore. I was just Jack.

"You're home. You're finally home. I thought I'd never see you again."

"Gertrude?" She was the same age when I last saw her seventy-four years ago. Just as beautiful as I remembered, too.

"Forgot me already?"

"I never forgot you." Was that true? I had blocked out much of my pre-Pandemonium life. It was the only way to survive, but this world also makes you forget. It eats up your sweet memories. I remembered Gertie for the first time in many years when Zara gave me the water of remembering back in the Duke's palace. The memory was so painful I had to repress it again. But with her standing before me, it all flooded back, and talking to her—even a fake version—came easily and naturally.

"I never forgot you, Jack. I waited and waited. And now you're here."

She embraced me. I expected her arms to go through me like a ghost, but her warm and solid arms clutched me tight, the first human being I had touched in decades. I had to admit it felt good.

She led me to the couch and we sat.

"What year is it?" I asked.

"You really had a rough time, didn't you, sweetie? It's 1946."

Glenn Miller changed to the Lemon Sisters.

"Who won the war?"

"You don't know?"

"Refresh my memory."

"We did."

"No more Nazis?"

She looked at me like she didn't understand.

"Jack, do you feel well? I'll bring you a drink and food. Are you still drinking whiskey?"

"This isn't real. You're not real."

"Don't be silly.

"I'm as real as you are."

I looked at my hands and nice, clean suit. "I don't think I'm all that real."

"I'll fix you up and you'll be fine."

She walked over to the credenza. Next to the radio sat several bottles of alcohol and a couple of glasses, just like our old apartment in Brooklyn. She poured me a drink, then took a small plate out from one of the drawers. When she returned, she handed me the glass and plate. On the plate were chocolate chip cookies, freshly baked from the smell. I nearly cried.

I put the plate on the couch between us and held the whiskey.

"Gertie, I'd love to believe you're really here, but you're no doubt no long dead."

"Don't talk like that, Jack. I thought for a long time you were dead. I hadn't heard from you in so long, and now here you are."

"Gertie, I have been long dead."

She laughed. "You don't look dead."

"This is an illusion. This is some elaborate magic trick."

"You're wrong, Jack. Ratzinger doesn't control the tower. The tower has been here before him and it will be here long after him."

"What do you know about the tower and Ratzinger?"

"I don't want to talk about that. I want to talk about us. Aren't you happy to see me? Aren't you happy to be home?"

"I am." And I meant it. I was human, even if an illusion, and I had my Gertie back.

"You can stay with me," she said. "We can be together. Isn't that what you want?" She reached down between the cushions of the couch and pulled out a gun, the same one from the dust den—a fat, cartoon revolver that could give the absolute death to a supernatural.

"We can be together," Gertie said. "Join me." She placed the gun in my hand. "You've never been happy here. Isn't it time to leave?"

"You want me to kill myself?"

"I want you to do the right thing. You don't have a soul. You lost the homunculus. You're alone and miserable. Now you have a chance to be with me and be human again. Why wouldn't you take it?"

"It isn't real."

"It's as real as anything else."

"I can't kill myself without my soul. I'll go to the depths of hell."

"Not if you do it here. This is a special place. You die here, you stay here. Live any way you like, free from all the horrors out there. I've never lied to you before, Jack."

Dead Jack and the Soul Catcher

Her green eyes shone in the darkness. She held my hand in hers. It felt warm, good. Very good. Gertie smiled an encouraging smile and stroked my human hand.

She was right, wasn't she? My existence in Pandemonium these past seventy-plus years had been torture, and the last few months had been unbearable. I had thought of killing myself before, but I had never taken it seriously until Oswald had fallen asleep. It was like I had fallen into a deep, dark hole that deepened as I struggled to escape. I had never felt more soulless. Even the dust and Devil Boy didn't fill the void. I put the barrel to my temple. Gertie smiled painfully.

Just a quick pull on the trigger.

I thought of Oswald. If I killed myself, what would happen to him? How could I enjoy a life, even a fake life, with Gertie, knowing Oswald was a Nazi stooge?

I put the gun down. "I can't, Gertie. You're a lie. This whole place is a lie for Ratzinger's benefit. He'd never let me rest."

"Why don't you eat, honey? I made them for you." She held the plate up.

The cookies had disappeared. Instead, a juicy, wet heart throbbed on the plate. Thick, purple veins crisscrossed its translucent skin. I jumped back.

"It looks good, doesn't it?" Gertie picked up the beating heart. She put it to her mouth and bit into it, blood smearing her lips.

"Gertie, no!" I stood, backing away.

"You were always a coward, Jack." Gertie's green eyes turned black. She tried to grab my hand, but I pulled away.

"A fookin, no-good coward," she said. "I'm glad I'm dead and everyone you ever loved, too."

I turned away from Gertie, my heart burning, and walked back into the darkness.

She wasn't real, I told myself, only part of Ratzinger's mind games, and the worst part hadn't even come yet. I knew what awaited me on the next level, and I didn't know if I would survive it.

I had visited Room 731 many, many times in my nightmares, reliving its terrors. But the real nightmare was up there. Ratzinger in the flesh.

I mounted the staircase, the spotlight lighting my way to the cherry on top of this shit cake that was the Obsidian Tower.

Suicide-inducing gray walls, bloodstained floors, the room appeared exactly as I remembered. The metal chair. The cold steel tables. The rack of surgical tools. The smell of human fear.

Wet hands clapped, like a seal slapping its flippers together.

"Welcome home, 1-1-3-4."

The voice stabbed my heart like a knife. I searched the room, but didn't see the Nazi bastard.

"I knew you'd return. You were always a determined creature. But don't all zombies have to be?"

"Have you gotten shy, Ratzinger? I'd like to see your face. It's been awhile. Are you still as ugly?"

Nervous laughter.

"I'm not alone. I've brought a friend."

A shadowy figure appeared in the far left corner of the room. It unfolded itself and moved toward me with visible effort. The thing walked worse than a three-legged sphinx.

It moved into the light. I'd like to say I took it well. I'd like to say I didn't scream. Or bile didn't rise into the back of my mouth. I think I tasted Fine Flanagan again. The figure didn't turn out to be Ratzinger. It was the Duke. He looked worse for wear. The last time I saw him, he was somersaulting over the side of Skull Mountain. I assumed, as we all did, that he had died in the fall. As I looked at his ashen face and sunken eyes, I thought my assumption still correct. His once-robust body was drawn and slight, as if his insides had been sucked out. His black Nazi uniform drooped around his emaciated frame.

"Still hiding, Ratzinger? Did you age badly? Are you fat and bald?"

"It is much worse than that." The voice came from behind the Duke. Was he hiding behind his new lackey?

The Duke turned, exposing a gray blob-like mass that protruded from the left side of his abdomen, through a slit in his tunic. Like a giant tumor with a dagger slash for a mouth. But his eyes were the same—one blue-white, the other nearly black—and he still had that little Hitler mustache.

"Sadly, I am not complete," the thing said in Ratzinger's voice. Tiny veins throbbed under his paper-thin skin. "Eddie was kind enough to lend me his body as I—well, as I grow. When the Children of Thule resurrected me, I was nothing but essence. But that wonderful Ilsa—what a mind on her!—had been doing such splendid work with hybrids and discovered a way to bring me back in corporeal form. In time, I will consume Eddie and have a body all my own."

"That's disgusting. I might need to vomit. I've seen some truly disgusting things in my life, but you are the most hideous creature I've ever laid eyes on."

"Well, you are no Rudolph Valentino yourself."

"You look like a tumor that gave birth to a bunch of older tumors."

"I am not at my final stage. I will improve."

"You look like you belong in a zoo for tumors. You look like a tumor that ate a tumor and shit out you. You look like something a blind dwarf would have made if someone explained to him what a tumor looked like."

"I get it. You think I look like a tumor. As I already said, I am in the process of—"

"Becoming a bigger tumor?"

The thing scowled. "I have your soul, arsehole. It was jumping like a jitterbug while you were ascending the tower."

"Is that why you had me go through all that mental fookery?"

"I needed to see how far you have come. You have been out in the wild for so long, you have developed some will-power. A nasty thing for a zombie. You are not meant to think for yourself."

"And you'll take care of that for me, will you?"

"Jack, you fool, you have never done any of your own thinking. I studied your little comrade before we put him to work upstairs." Ratzinger pointed at the ceiling with a tiny finger—little more than a nub sticking out from his tumor-body. "He has come in so handy. Speaking of hands…Eddie, would you mind opening yours?"

Still looking off into space, without blinking, the Duke held up his right fist, opened it. In his palm, he held an egg-sized vessel. I knew what was inside it.

"All these years you yearned for your soul," Ratzinger said, "and it was right next to you the entire time. Do you understand irony?"

Hearing it made it real. How long did I know? Maybe from the time Oswald took up residence in my skull. I didn't know. Ever since he showed up, I felt like a missing piece of myself had been found. And maybe that's why I resented him for so long. He was the better part of me.

"That homunculus has been doing your thinking for you," Ratzinger said. "Don't you see? You found another master. It is your nature. It is who you are."

"What did you do with Oswald?"

"He is safe. As safe as one can be inside a soul sucker. The poor thing not only held the universe's most powerful energy source, he had to lug around your heavy soul. I do not know how he did it. But he has been unburdened."

The Duke placed the soul vessel over Ratzinger's ugly mouth and the Nazi doctor swallowed it in one gulp. When he spoke, I heard the words in my mind. 1-1-3-4, please take a seat.

I dutifully walked over to the steel chair in the middle of the room. He had no need to tie me up. I sat still like a good zombie. As long as Ratzinger had my soul, he had my obedience. I was trapped inside my own mind.

"You have been a naughty boy, 1-1-3-4. I will forgive you, but you need to be punished. You remember our little games during the war?"

When I saw the red gas can, I didn't react, couldn't react. Somewhere deep inside, I screamed.

The Duke crossed the room and picked up the gas can. Ratzinger rubbed his little nub hands together.

The Duke/Ratzinger hybrid stood before me. Ratzinger looked more hideous up close, his skin alligator rough and bumpy. His tiny veins pulsed.

"You should thank me for burning your filthy suit and

hat," he said. "We'll fix you up with a new Children of Thule uniform."

The Duke lifted the gas can, but before he could dump its contents over my head, something came whistling through the air, struck the gas can, and sent it flying.

The distraction was enough for Ratzinger to momentarily lose his grip on me, and I gained the ability to turn my head. Zara stood beside a steel table, her silver hammer in her hand. Ilsa Hellstrom's head rolled to a stop at my feet, her little Nazi hat still affixed to her skull. She winked at me. The bodiless bitch lived.

"What the fook happened to you, Eddie?" Zara said.

"Eddie isn't home," Ratzinger said.

"Who the fook are you? What the fook are you? Screw it." Zara charged, her hammer leading the way. The Duke ran toward his ex. She leaped, swinging the hammer at the Duke's head. He moved with surprising swiftness, sidestepping at the last second.

"Jack, why are you just sitting there!" Zara shouted.

I wanted to answer her, I wanted to move, but I couldn't do a damn thing.

The Duke picked up an electric bone saw. It whirred to life, the small circular blade spinning as he made quick jabbing motions at her.

"This time I'm going to kill you dead," Zara said, "and that giant pimple of yours."

"We have not been introduced," the malformed man said in a calm voice. "My name is Dr. Josef Ratzinger. And you must be Zara Moonbeam. From the looks of you, you must have one healthy, delicious soul. I am going to enjoy sucking it up."

"How many psycho Nazi doctors are there in this place?"

The Duke hurled the saw at Zara and it tore into her left thigh. Blood shot out in short, violent bursts. She stumbled back several steps, but managed to remain standing. The Duke grabbed a long scalpel and lunged at Zara. Before she went down, she raised her hammer handle sideways to block. He landed on top of her, pushing down the hammer handle, the scalpel still in his right hand. Ratzinger bent down and, like a leech, attached his lipless mouth to her bleeding wound. Zara howled in pain.

As Ratzinger drank, he again lost his grip on me. I didn't hesitate. I jumped out of the steel chair and kicked the Duke as hard as I could in the ribs. He flipped onto his side, crushing Ratzinger. The doctor cried out in pain. The scalpel fell out of the Duke's hand and stuck in Zara's upper chest.

"Ratzinger is controlling the Duke," I said. "Cut him loose."

The pixie/witch yanked out the scalpel and slashed Ratzinger. He let out another sharp cry. Zara gripped the scalpel tighter and dug deep into his flesh, dragging the razor-sharp tool down, until she severed Ratzinger from the giant body. The little tumor-man vomited up my soul egg, which rolled across the room.

Ratzinger scurried away like a bloated worm and hid under a surgical table. Without his Nazi tumor, the Duke didn't move. Zara jumped to her feet and brought her hammer down onto his head. His skull caved in with a sickening crunch, his right eye popping out and dangling from its stalk. Screaming in rage, she brought the hammer down again and again, until only a bloody pulp remained.

Apparently, she wanted to make sure they didn't re-resurrect him.

Something clattered. The talking tumor was on the move. Ratzinger had climbed up the wall, blood dripping from his bottom half. I scooped up my soul jar and stuffed it in my pocket. Then I grabbed the gas can and approached him from the left. Zara took the right.

"You don't really want to live like an abomination, do you?" I said. "You should see yourself. People will laugh at you and you seem to have a fragile ego."

"You will pay for this," Ratzinger said.

"Is that the best you can do?"

"The things I did to you will be nothing compared to what I will visit upon you and that witch."

The overgrown Nazi zit scurried farther up the wall, its slimy body sticking to the surface like glue.

"Fire good," I said, and drenched the Nazi. The sickly sweet smell of gas filled the room.

Ratzinger went nuts, crawling onto the ceiling and hightailing it away from us. I frantically searched for my lighter, found it, and flicked on the flame.

"Wish me luck," I muttered to Zara.

"Luck," she said.

I chucked the lighter at Ratzinger, the flame spinning end over end. It hit the ceiling and skipped right into the little bugger. Whoosh! He squealed as the flames cooked him. The tumor bucked and twisted, finally dropping to the floor. Somehow, he still moved, a flaming ball of hate, scurrying on the ground like, well, a man on fire. He crashed into a wooden chest, which went up in flames like dry newspaper. Then he ran into a cabinet, which also went up in flames. Pretty soon, flames engulfed the entire room.

Ratzinger disappeared into the billowing smoke.

Zara ran toward the smoke.

"We need to get to Oswald," I said. "Forget Ratzinger."

Zara turned back. "Where is he?"

I pointed at the ceiling.

But there seemed to be no way out of the room. I didn't see a staircase leading to the top of the tower, and the one leading to this level had vanished once I entered.

"We can't get up there," I said.

"You just have to imagine a staircase," Zara said. "The tower conjures up your thoughts. That's how I got up here."

"How did you get in the tower in the first place?"

"Ilsa told me. She was friendly after I chopped off her head."

Ilsa? I had almost forgotten about her. I scanned the floor for the Nazi's severed head, but it had disappeared. I had no time to worry about her. I thought of a staircase, concentrated, closed my eyes, and when I opened them, there appeared a flight of stone steps leading to the top of the tower.

"Good work, Jack," Zara said.

We mounted the stairs, black clouds of smoke rising with us, flames licking at our feet.

If I had conjured the stairs, did I conjure all the other things I faced in the Obsidian Tower? Was I torturing myself, not Ratzinger? What was I going to find atop the tower?

A red glow bathed the top floor up ahead. At first, I thought the flames had somehow gotten ahead of us, but when we emerged from the stairwell, I realized that the upper level had no roof, and the crimson glow came from the bloody Pandemonium sky.

In the middle of the roof sat a fifty-foot soul sucker. Heavy chains, anchored in the ground, were lashed around its legs. The creature looked like a cross between a giant vulture and a seagull, its great mouth thrown open at an ninety-degree angle, its sharp beak pointing straight up at the sky.

Orbs of purple and yellow and blue light streamed from all over Pandemonium directly into the creature's waiting maw. Its bloated brown belly grew fatter and fatter with souls.

"Where exactly is Oswald?" Zara said.

"Inside that thing."

I circled the eyeless creature—it didn't seem to notice our presence—and discovered a red, swollen scar in its chest.

"Do you still have the scalpel?" I asked Zara.

"Right here." She handed me the surgical tool.

I cut around the scar, the scalpel catching in the soul sucker's rough, leathery skin. The creature didn't stir as green blood seeped out of the wound. It kept on eating up souls as if it felt nothing. I cut a hole as big as my head in the sucker's chest and punched my fist through the opening, feeling around its warm insides. My arm was nearly elbow deep when I touched Oswald's smooth, rubbery skin. I grabbed him by the foot and yanked, but didn't get far. My arm stuck as the creature's wound sealed around it. I tried to pull it out, but it wouldn't budge.

"Zara, gut this fook."

I went to work with the scalpel on the soul sucker to free myself.

Zara lifted her hammer—and fell flat on her face. The soul sucker had awoken and swung its thick, fleshy tail into the back of the witch's head.

Dead Jack and the Soul Catcher

She rose onto her hands and knees, and the creature's tail slammed into her stomach, sending her under the soul sucker.

I slashed and tore through the monster, green blood showering me. I pulled out my arm as the soul sucker bucked and thrashed.

I held Oswald, green goo dripping off him. The Jupiter Stone burned brightly inside his limp and lifeless body. The behemoth let out a piercing scream as it jackhammered its tail into the floor. The tower shook and I backed toward the edge.

Then soul sucker whimpered, slumped, and fell on its side. The beast's mouth shut like a steel trap, and the lights in the sky disappeared. Its underbelly glowed bright white, then tore open in a torrent of multicolored light pouring from its body.

Zara emerged from under the creature, holding a wet dagger. A huge smile spread across her face.

"I'd applaud," I said, "but my hands are full."

Zara stepped toward the staircase. Flames shot up from the level below and smoke poured out of the tower like a Lucky Dragon factory had exploded below.

"We need to get off this tower," she said. "And we can't go down there."

I peered over the edge and stared at the thousand-foot drop. "Oswald could make it." I turned, holding up the ball of fluff. The Jupiter Stone's glow faded. The little guy looked deader than ever.

"Oswald doesn't look like he's going to be much help," Zara said.

"I can bring him back."

"How?"

"I have our soul."

"Our soul? Isn't it your soul?"

"No. It hasn't been my soul for a long time. He's done much better with it than I ever did."

"I'm confused."

"I'll tell you all about it when this is all over."

I removed the soul egg from my pocket, cracked it open, and sucked up my soul. But I didn't swallow.

"Jack, wouldn't you—"

I held up a finger, cutting her off. I pried open Oswald's mouth, leaned toward the homunculus, and blew into his mouth. His body filled with a bright purple light and then dissolved back to the color of a marshmallow. Oswald still lay in my hands, lifeless and unresponsive. I shook him. But he just jiggled like a bowl of gelatin.

Was I wrong? I knew I shouldn't have trusted hallucinations while high on dust. This whole time Oswald really was just a figment of my imagination. I finally understood what he meant when he said I'd known all along and couldn't admit it. He was dead. Oswald was gone and never coming back.

I should have listened to Gertie. No, I should have blown my brains out back in the dust den and saved myself all this trouble.

"We have to go," Zara said.

I wiped the green goo off Oswald. "I'm staying."

"Are you crazy?"

"Go without me."

"You'll burn to ashes if you stay."

"Don't you get it? Oswald's dead. Really dead."

"Oswald's been dead a long time. You tried, Jack. You did everything you could, but we have to get off this tower before it turns back to lava."

An inferno raged around us. The tower softened, its glass surface turning into goo.

"He was more than my best friend," I said. "He was—"

Oswald's limbs went rigid. His X eyes blinked. He coughed.

"Finish what you were going to say," the homunculus said in a sleepy voice.

Something caught in my throat, and I couldn't speak. I gagged. "I was going to say it took you damn long enough to wake up. We're about an inch from death here."

"I've heard everything you've been saying."

"So? You know I'm a liar."

"And a dust head and a coward and my best friend."

"Don't make me regret saving your life, Oswald. I can take my soul back any time."

"This changes everything, you know?"

"You're not going to let me live this down, are you?"

Oswald smiled.

"Guys, the fire?" Zara said. "I don't want to interrupt the family reunion, but—"

"Zara," Oswald said. "How have you been?"

"Hi, Oswald. Let's catch up when we're not in imminent danger of being burned to death."

"Oswald, can you still morph?" I asked.

"I think I can do a lot more than that now," Oswald said.

"Don't brag. It's ugly."

I placed Oswald on the floor. He stretched his arms and legs, rolled his head around, arched his back. The Jupiter Stone flashed inside his chest.

I shook my head. "Geez, he's going to be impossible from now on."

Oswald spread out into a giant tarp. "Get on top of me."

As soon as we flopped down on top of him, Oswald curled up his body and enveloped us in a cushiony ball. "Hold on. We're going over the edge."

The giant Oswald ball rolled. Me and Zara tumbled like a pair of dice thrown in a high-stakes game of craps. We banged into the edge of the tower, went over it, and floated weightless.

"Oswald knows what he's doing, right?" Zara asked.

I didn't answer.

We plummeted a thousand feet in silence.

My neck cracked when we hit the ground, but I only needed to pop it back in place. It didn't help that we bounced a hundred feet in the air. We kept bouncing, each time a bit lower, me and Zara crashing into each other, until Oswald slammed into a somewhat-hard surface and stopped moving. He unfurled himself, releasing us before morphing back to his usual homunculus shape. We'd wound up at the bottom of a ditch a couple hundred feet away from the tower.

"That was fun," he said. "Want to do it again?"

It dawned on me that Oswald might have lost a few marbles since he went into a coma.

22

DEAL OR NO DEAL

THREE QUICK EXPLOSIONS came from the east. Columns of black smoke blasted into the sky. Winged demons patrolled high over the camp. Every now and then, one would descend and a scream would follow. The roar of cannons and vehicles had ceased.

Beleth rode his pale horse through the clouds in the middle of the sky. He flicked his wand from side to side, screams ringing out to the discordant beat of his infernal soundtrack.

"If we can find a car, we can drive to Magus Cove and catch a ghost ship—a reputable ghost ship—off Witch End," I said.

"You want to take a ghost ship?" Oswald asked. "After our adventure in the Broken Sea, I thought you said you'd never travel in a ghost ship again."

"I've gotten much braver since you took your big nap."

"Hellstrom's Mercedes is probably still there," Zara said, "but don't you have to settle things with Lucifer?"

"We didn't have anything in writing."

"You made a deal with Lucifer?" Oswald asked. "I've been away for a little while and you're already making Faustian bargains?"

"I did it for you, dunzy. Had you woken up sooner, we wouldn't be in this situation."

"What was the deal?"

"I don't want to say."

"He promised him the Jupiter Stone and The Book of Three Towers," Zara said.

Oswald shook his head. The homunculus was still a judgmental thing.

"Relax," I said. "I didn't mean to give him anything. I had my fingers crossed."

The car still idled in the clearing midway between the tower and the edge of camp. Nazi Town was completely ablaze now. Beleth and his legions had created a new hell. The Obsidian Tower, too, melted like a giant Popsicle. Giant tendrils of flame shot from its peak.

"Let's hurry," I said.

We had made it to the car when I smelled brimstone. In a puff of smoke, Lucifer appeared. He wore Bermuda shorts, a loose Hawaiian shirt, and sandals with black socks. Five thick-necked demons popped into existence behind him.

"I bet you were just on your way to see me," he said.

"I figured you'd pop up," I said.

"We had a deal. Remember? Give me the homunculus."

"You gave me up?" Oswald said. "And I believed that stuff you said about me. The nice stuff, I mean."

"Don't get all sentimental," I said. "He only wants the Jupiter Stone. He wants to remove it and then he'll return you safe and sound. Isn't that right?"

"And The Book of Three Towers," Lucifer said.

Oswald shook his head. "Nope."

"Did he just say nope?" Lucifer said.

"I didn't make a deal with you," Oswald said.

Lucifer laughed. "This little man has some big balls. Do I need to remind you both that when you have a contract with the Devil, you don't negotiate."

"We don't have a contract," I said. "There's nothing in writing."

"We have a verbal agreement. That's a legally binding deal where I come from."

"There are extenuating circumstances."

"Which are?"

"I don't want to make the deal anymore."

"It doesn't work like that."

"I discovered that Oswald owns my soul."

"That sounds very romantic, but you two should keep that to yourselves."

Lucifer approached Oswald.

The Jupiter Stone burned inside his chest, lighting him with an otherworldly glow. The homunculus expanded like an inflating tire.

"What's he doing?" Lucifer said.

"I think you're getting him mad," I said.

"Jack may have made an idiotic deal with you," Oswald said, his voice smooth and deep. Nothing pipsqueak about it. "But I certainly did not."

"A deal's a fookin deal!" Lucifer got a bit hysterical. He stamped his feet and smoke shot out of his ears. "Why do people think they can always get out of deals with the Devil? It's unbelievable. Do I look like an idiot? Is this the face of an idiot?" He pointed at his face. "We had a deal.

You agreed to it. I upheld my end of the bargain. Is it too much to ask people to act fairly?"

"There's no deal," Oswald said.

The Jupiter Stone inside the homunculus burned a bright pink and a blue emanation enveloped his body, now twice its normal size.

"Don't mess with the bull unless you want the horns," Lucifer said. He directed his minions to grab Oswald. That was the last thing I saw. Oswald burned brighter, going from pink to orange to blue. An explosion of intense white light blinded me momentarily. When I got my eyesight back, Lucifer and his minions were gone. I looked toward the camp and I didn't see any demons in the sky either.

"What did you do, Oswald?" I asked.

Before he could answer, the wind picked up. It whipped through the clearing like a tornado. I had to grab my hat before it flew off. The burning tower rumbled and swayed like a licorice stick. Then, in a blink, it fell in on itself, collapsing and disappearing into the ground. Great puffs of smoke and debris shot into the air.

"What the fook did you do, Oswald?"

The homunculus said nothing.

We all stared at the spot where the Obsidian Tower had been. When the dust had settled, only a giant hole in the ground remained, with a swirling vortex at the bottom. Probably the worst kind of vortex there is.

"Oswald, whatever it is you're doing, stop," I said.

The homunculus had returned to his former size and shape. "I didn't do that." He pointed at the vortex. "I don't think I did, anyway. This is all new to me."

"Great. You have super powers now, but you're still an idiot. We're fookin doomed."

"I took care of that stupid deal you made. You should thank me."

"You killed Lucifer. There has to be repercussions for that."

"I didn't kill him. I just sent him back to hell."

"You what now?"

"He won't be bothering us anymore."

"You should have killed him, dunzy. Oh, geez, what did you do?"

"How about, 'Thank you, Oswald, for again saving the world and your arse and fixing your stupid plans.'"

"Do you really think you just saved us? When Lucifer gets back, what do you think he's going to do to us?"

"I thought no one could leave Pandemonium," Zara said.

"Are you sure you sent him to Hell?" I asked.

"That's where I willed him. I can send you there, too, and you can see if he made it."

"Oswald, you're talking out of your arse. And you've gotten quite sassy since you got that Jupiter Stone."

"I think the vortex is a portal out of Pandemonium," Oswald said.

"You created a cosmic toilet bowl and flushed Lucifer down the drain. Oswald, you might be a weapon of mass destruction, but you haven't changed a bit. You're nothing but a nuisance."

"That makes sense," Zara said. "We found an Angel Door in the Lucifer Tower. Maybe Oswald opened something like that in the Obsidian Tower. Can't you check with The Book of Three Towers?"

"Now you're asking me for answers," I said. "I thought super-homunculus had all the insights."

"You're just being ugly now." Oswald folded his arms.

"I do not like the new you." I took out the book, but just as I had thought, it had gone back to normal. No secret text about the towers. No help. Nothing. "Looks like without the tower, the book isn't accessing its location specific textuality. It's worthless now. Thanks, Oswald."

I looked at the swirling vortex, dark blue light spinning inside an infinitely deep sea of night. I didn't like it one bit. Trouble lurked in that unholy maelstrom.

"Can the portal reach the Other World?" I asked.

"I don't know," Oswald said, "but I can't see why not."

"Great. Now monsters can take a holiday in New Jersey. Wasn't that why we stopped the Pandemonium Device? We're back at square one."

"No," Zara said. "We stopped the device to stop the destruction of Pandemonium. Not everyone likes being trapped here, you know."

"Speaking for yourself?"

"I'm happy here, but my father always wanted to go back home. And I think he should have had that choice. This might be a good thing."

"I seriously doubt that. Look at it."

"Guys, I don't want to alarm anyone," Oswald said.

"Why care now? I'm really starting to regret giving you my soul."

"I was just thinking. If things could go out, couldn't things come in, too?"

"How the heck are we supposed to know?" I screamed. "You created this thing. Why are you asking us questions?"

"Can you make it disappear, Oswald?" Zara asked.

"I can try."

Oswald stared at the vortex. His X eyes flattened to

horizontal lines. He did his glowing and puffing up bit. Me and Zara and backed up. Who knew if he'd managed to blow us all up. Or if Lucifer would jump out of the dark depths and kill us both. Oswald didn't seem to have much of a handle on the stone's power.

The swirling vortex doubled in size.

Lucifer was right about him being a ticking time bomb. He would destroy the entire dimension if given the chance.

"How is he doing that?" I asked. "He's doing the exact worst thing possible. Stop, Oswald. I forbid you to use the power of the Jupiter Stone. You're cut off! Done!"

The homunculus shrank, his glow dimmed.

The vortex now swirled at least half a mile wide.

"I can't do it," Oswald said. "I don't think I can get rid of it."

"I wish you knew that before you made it bigger," I said. "I think the vortex is swirling faster, too."

"Do you know how you created it?" Zara asked.

"Not really. It just sort of happened."

"We can't just leave it here," I said. "We need to hide it."

"I can create a glamour, but it won't be very strong. Anyone who investigates will see that it's an illusion."

"With the Nazis dead or gone, this place will hopefully stay vacant for a while. We just need enough time to figure what to do."

Zara stood at the edge of the vortex. She mumbled some arcane words as she traced figures in the air. Soon, the Obsidian Tower—or a reasonable facsimile—had appeared over the spot.

"It's as thin as a whisper," she said. "I know some witches on Witch End who can guard the tower and keep up the glamour."

"Do you know anyone who sells dust, too?" I deserved it

23

HOW DO YOU SOLVE A PROBLEM LIKE OSWALD?

OSWALD WANTED TO transport us back to ShadowShade with his newfound power, but I stuck to my new rule: Oswald never uses the Jupiter Stone again. He can't even be trusted with filing. Since he'd become sorcerer supreme, I trembled at the mere sight of him. But it wasn't his power that got on my nerves so much as his ego. He strutted around like he owned Pandemonium. And he wouldn't let the soul thing go. He kept making goo-goo eyes at me, like a lovesick teenager.

"You're creeping me out. Where's my dust?" I flipped through the ShadowShade Sentinel looking for any stories about the Nazi camp or the Obsidian Tower. I was exhausted. I needed to take a six-month nap like Oswald or a good bump of dust. It was usually as good as a vacation. I sat behind my desk. Oswald sat in front of the typewriter, ineptly banging out a report.

"I got rid of it," he said.

"If you used your cosmic powers, I'm taking back my soul."

"I told you to stop using the stuff, and I meant it. If I can't use the Jupiter Stone, you can't use dust. Didn't you learn anything in the Obsidian Tower?"

"I learned that you're a menace to society."

"Don't make me use my hoodoo." The homunculus held up a hand, as if to hex me.

Maybe I should listen to him. He could wish me into another dimension.

"That's not funny. You got sadistic since you became a demi-god. Remember, I gave you life."

Zara had headed back to Fairy Land to see if she could learn anything about the portal and if we could do anything about it. I told her not to give away too much info. We needed to keep the vortex a secret. No telling what would happen if word got out. Fortunately, I didn't see anything about it in the paper, though an article about a giant spider terrorizing a downtown café had made page two. We left a few human witches Zara trusted to guard the tower and keep up the glamour. So far, it had been quiet. But rumors swirled that the Children of Thule regrouped on the Zombie Islands. I had no doubt Ratzinger still scurried about, and his gal pal Ilsa, too, even if she was just a head. I had a feeling Nazis more powerful than those two pulled the strings. I couldn't stop thinking about that werewolf Hitler statue. I hoped it was only a bad artistic decision, but Nazis like to bring nightmares to life. It's their modus operandi.

"Do you really think you opened a portal?" I asked.

"There's only one way to find out."

"You can't be serious. This is home. The Other World is no place for us, believe me. They'd hate you. And I don't think Hell would be an improvement over Pandemonium."

"I think it would be interesting to travel. The real Coney Island sounds like so much fun. I'd like to eat a hot dog."

"Finish your report. Does that Jupiter Stone make you spell any better? You still can't type worth a damn."

"You never put my name on the office door."

"There's something about this adventure that's still bugging me."

"How you got through it without eating anyone?"

"How did you know your way around the alchemist's labyrinth? You guided me through it perfectly."

The homunculus got quiet and stopped typing.

"Had you ever been there before?"

Oswald look up at the ceiling, as if in deep thought. "I did have a life before I met you."

"What do you know about 'alraun'? The dead alchemist mentioned it when I gave him dust."

"That's easy. Alraun is mandrake."

"I know that, dunzy."

"Why would he say a mandrake killed him?"

"Because it did."

"How would you know that?"

"Because I was the mandrake. I killed him."

"You what?"

Lilith floated through the door.

"Lil, can't you open the door just once?" I said. "We're in the middle of something."

"Ms. Moonbeam is here and—"

But the pixie/witch didn't wait to be let in. She threw open the door.

"That portal is trouble," she said, her face pale and worried.

"Tell me something I don't know."

She stood in front of my desk. "No, Jack, you don't know. When Oswald zapped Lucifer back to hell, he created a huge problem in Pandemonium. The devil was the only thing keeping the gangs from killing each other. He had forced a truce between the Five Families. With him gone, they're going to war. They're going to rip Pandemonium apart."

"I knew I should have thrown Oswald in that damn swirling vortex when I had the chance."

"That's not all. Remember when Oswald asked what if things came through the portal? Well, something got through. Something big."

"Lilith, call all the dust dealers in town. Tell them money is no problem."

Looks like I picked a hell of a time to go straight.

COMING SOON...
Dead Jack and the Old Gods (Book 3)

Acknowledgments

TWELVE YEARS AGO, I wrote the first Dead Jack story, "The Case of the Amorous Ogre." Convinced no one wanted to read a zombie detective story, I filed it away and forgot about it. Five years later, in 2011, I took my first and (so far) last fiction writing class. We were required to submit two short stories for review. My first, a dark, literary attempt at magic realism, was an embarrassing disaster. The second planned story hadn't been finished by the deadline. I thought of skipping the assignment, but then I remembered the zombie detective story buried somewhere on my hard drive. I dug it out, but it was over the word limit. So, just before the deadline, I cut a scene where Oswald, then a worm named Ollie, takes over the narrative and heroically travels by helicopter to Black Rock. I uploaded it and waited for the inevitable scathing reviews. But days later, the class, even the aloof instructor, raved about it. They wanted to see a Dead Jack series, they wanted more. Could my unwarranted pessimism have been wrong? I tested that possibility a few months later, when I submitted the story to Weird Tales Magazine. "The Case of the Amorous Ogre" became my first story acceptance. Four years later, in 2016, I would run a Kickstarter campaign for the first novel in the series, *Dead Jack and the Pandemonium Device*. It would be optioned for a film and TV series. And here we are. With Book 2, *Dead Jack and the Soul Catcher*, in your words. Apparently, people do want to read about a zombie detective. Fook pessimism!

I couldn't have done it alone. Over the years, plenty of people have helped the series get this far. I'd like to thank Weird Tales and Marvin Kaye for accepting my first short story and getting this thing off.

Editor Matthew S. Cox gave me a much needed kick in the butt and helped make *Dead Jack and the Soul Catcher* kick ass.

Producers Tony Eldridge, Gloria Morrison, and John Harlacher have done so much more than option my work. They've encouraged and supported the series from the beginning. It's much appreciated.

Book 2 again has amazing art from Colton Worley (cover art), Ed Watson (interior art), and Shawn King (cover design). These guys rock!

And a bigger thank-you to my biggest fan and supporter, my darling wife, Jennifer!

ABOUT THE AUTHOR

JAMES AQUILONE WAS raised on Saturday morning cartoons, comic books, sitcoms, and Cap'n Crunch. Amid the Cold War, he dreamed of being a jet fighter pilot but decided against the military life after realizing it would require him to wake up early. He had further illusions of being a stand-up comedian, until a traumatic experience on stage forced him to seek a college education. Brief stints as an alternative rock singer/guitarist and child model also proved unsuccessful. Today he battles a severe chess addiction while trying to write in the speculative fiction game.

His first novel, *Dead Jack and the Pandemonium Device*, has been optioned for film and television. His short fiction has been published in such places as Nature Futures, *The Best of Galaxy's Edge 2013-2014*, *Unidentified Funny Objects 4*, and Weird Tales Magazine. Suffice it to say, things are going much better than his modeling career.

He lives in Staten Island, New York, with his wonderful wife.

THANK YOU FOR READING

Now that you've finished *Dead Jack and the Soul Catcher*, please leave a review. It won't kill you.

For more info, go to DeadJack.com

Printed in Great Britain
by Amazon